LOVE WALKS IN

LISA MONDELLO

FOREWORD

Being able to make a living doing what you love is a blessing. But even blessings have their struggles. It's been several years since I released a new book because life has had a funny way of dumping all its blessings and struggles together in one big heap. The pain of losing a parent either suddenly or over a period is something almost all of us have experienced or will experience.

When my dad became ill with cancer, my siblings and I took turns flying to Florida to help him and his wife through a year of treatments and setbacks. We each made several trips that year, spreading them out so my dad and his wife would have help. The end is always heartbreaking even when there is relief that the pain is over. But there were many blessings along the way in the time we all got to spend with my father. We always had great conversations about books, movies, stories, the classics and politics. He wanted me to read Moby Dick to him on his deathbed and I dutifully did, even though I did complain that it had taken an entire chapter for Ishmael to find a hotel room in New Bedford. Having grown up in the town next to New Bedford, I thought it was odd. That sort of remark usually led to a forty-five-minute conversation about writing.

He was a champion in my quest to become a writer. Early on, he said to me, "Don't say you're going to be a writer, Lisa. Say, I *am* a writer." I would always remember this when I was having a particularly hard time writing a scene just to remind myself. We talked about my books all the time and there was no doubt that he was proud of me.

Just months after my father's death, I learned I had cancer. I was lucky it was caught early, and I am now cancer free. But I'd barely had time to grieve my father's death when I heard the news and then didn't have time to work through my grief until I was finished with surgery. And then my sister got ill and needed to live with me for a while. Add having my now three-year-old grandson living with us while my daughter worked through her own grief after his father passed away when he was just nine weeks old, and well, suffice to say, my plate was full. A dump of blessings and struggles. There were many, many blessings along the way, but my hectic life made it difficult to think about plotting a romance, much less writing one.

Fast forward to December 2023 and I learned of the 80s Mixtape series that was being put together. I loved the 80s. I graduated high school in the 80s. I managed a rock band in Boston in the 80s. I went to awesome concerts in the 80s. I met my husband in the 80s. This was my jam. I jumped on the opportunity to be a part of this series. I'd been struggling to write, and I knew this series would bring my passion back to life. And it did. I thoroughly enjoyed writing LOVE WALKS IN. I loved writing about characters who are closer to my age and have lived a little. I loved revisiting memories.

As I wrote LOVE WALKS IN, a story centering around a high school reunion, I realized the proximity of the story in the fictitious coastal town of Crystal Cove was so close to the *El Faro* memorial in Dames Point Park in Jacksonville, Fl. It hit me like a ton of bricks. Sadly, one of my high school classmates, Mariette Wright, went down with the *El Faro* when it was lost at sea on October 1, 2015, during Hurricane Joaquin. It was a great shock to all who knew her. I realized I couldn't write this book, a story about a class reunion, without somehow paying homage to Mariette. In LOVE WALKS IN, there is a scene mentioning a character named Marie who died on the *El Faro*. She doesn't exist. So, if you ever visit the memorial and look down at the column of names, you won't find a Marie. I made her up. You will find Mariette Wright's name. I hadn't seen Mariette since high school, but I remember she loved Pete Townsend and The Who back in the day. I learned she loved the sea and working on ships. My only comfort in her family and friend's loss is that she died doing what she loved.

I hope you enjoy reading LOVE WALKS IN as much as I enjoyed writing it.

Many blessings,

Lisa Mondello

To my dad, Salvatore A. Mondello, 1937-2022
Hey, Dad, I am a writer!

~

As a hotel event planner at one of Crystal Cove's beach resorts, Meredith Prichard dreads the 1989 class reunion booked in Crystal Cove. Rumor has it Griffin Cole, the man who'd broken her heart by breaking their engagement to fight for his country during the Gulf War, will be there. The handsome, fun-loving man she'd fallen head over heels in love with in high school, was now a decorated Colonel in the Air Force. Faced with the past and the memories of their love, Meredith now questions returning to Crystal Cove when Griffin forces her to face the love between them that never died and the past decision Meredith made to forget him.

CHAPTER 1

"Quick. Hide me!"

The tall, lanky eighteen-year-old young man had spent the better part of an hour spreading white tablecloths on the banquet tables only to have to remove them and put purple tablecloths the bride, and her mother had picked out on them instead. Meredith thought they were a garish purple, chosen to match the bridesmaids' dresses, and it took Meredith forever to track them down through a party rental house. But the bride's mother loved the color and convinced her daughter to choose it.

"Wait. You want me to what?"

Meredith Prichard clutched many of the crisp white tablecloths they'd removed from the banquet tables and held them tight in her arms, ignoring that they'd need to be laundered before being used again and causing more work for the staff. There were bigger issues at play here.

"You heard me!"

A bewildered David, who recently graduated from

Crystal Cove High School, looked around and said, "Who am I hiding you from?"

"Edward."

She stopped moving and listened. The sound of her boss calling her name from out in the hallway was faint. If she was quick enough, she could slip out the side door and lose him.

"You're hiding from Mr. Mahoney? The hotel manager?"

"Yes, him. I don't want to talk to him now. How many more tablecloths are left? Never mind. You collect the rest and send them to laundry services. I'll bring these."

"But Mr. Mahoney never comes down to the banquet room unless—"

"He's looking for me. He's been in a mood ever since he lost the bid for the Crystal Cove Class of 1989 High School Reunion as if that was a big deal for the hotel. He's been following me around all day, nitpicking everything I do. I've been hiding from him ever since this morning." She squeezed another tablecloth into her arms and then suddenly stopped moving to listen.

Seeing her standing there like a statue, David stopped pulling tablecloths from the table and looked around.

The faint call of, "Has anyone seen Meredith?" floated into the banquet hall.

"Crap."

"I've got you. I'll take the rest," David said uncomfortably. Then he shrugged. "Sorry."

Her cell phone rang as she turned to take this load to the laundry facility. She didn't need to look at the caller ID to see that it was Edward, so she ignored it.

The tablecloths weren't David's fault. He worked in

maintenance, not catering. But he heard Meredith's shriek when she checked the banquet room and found the wrong tablecloths on the tables. The rest of the catering staff were busy with other tasks, on their phones, or somewhere else they weren't supposed to be when she needed them. But David immediately stepped in to help.

"I owe you one, David."

"It's okay."

She'd managed to get to the side door leading to the path that ran along the side of the building to the laundry room before she heard Edward yelling at her back.

"Damn," she whispered. There was no way she could pretend she hadn't heard him.

"Meredith," he called out as he walked quickly toward her. "I've been calling you for an hour. Why aren't you picking up the phone?"

"Um, we had a last-minute glitch that needed fixing. My hands were full. It's all good now."

He glanced around the banquet hall, which was nearly ready for the wedding that was about to take place in a few hours and grimaced as David spread the purple tablecloth on a banquet table.

"Whose idea was that?"

"Bride's choice."

Edward rolled his eyes and quickly turned toward her. "They're paying. They can have whatever damned color they want. Please tell me they were rented."

"They are."

"I have to talk with you about something."

"I'm really busy. Can it wait?"

"You have a handful of dirty tablecloths in your hands. How busy can you be?"

Irritation made its way up her spine. "Not dirty. Just the wrong color."

"I'm sure laundry can wait."

"This is the last thing I must do for tonight's wedding. It's going to go off without a hitch, and then I can get out of here right after the function is over for my two-week vacation."

"Yeah, about that. I'm going to need you to cancel your vacation and reschedule."

Her stomach dropped. "Excuse me?"

He put a smile on his face that she'd seen dozens of times before and hated. It usually meant he was ready to drop one of his fabulous ideas, which were awful, on her.

"The Ocean Vista is now officially an overflow hotel for the Crystal Cove High School Class of 1989 Reunion. I need you on-call all weekend."

"What is your obsession with this class reunion? And what exactly does this mean?"

Rocking back on his heels, he grinned. "When a big event happens, you must be part of it. We have a guest booked here for the reunion. That makes us overflow."

She held the tablecloths like they were her lifeline to sanity. He was actually serious. It was as if being the overflow for such a small local class reunion was a big deal. And maybe it was to Edward. He'd only been working as the manager of the Ocean Vista Hotel for a few months. To him, lining up the pencils face up in the Concierge desk box was a big deal.

"You want me to cancel my vacation for one guest?"

"People talk."

"They sure do. Edward, this is a local high school reunion. You're talking about one guest. It's hardly something the local papers will write about."

"Yours?"

"My what?"

"Your reunion. You grew up in Crystal Cove. I assume you graduated from Crystal Cove High School."

"A lot of people who work here did. David just graduated. I graduated two years after the Class of '89. Look, the Hawthorne House booked all the events for the reunion. The details are all set. Nothing is happening here. I should know. I book *all* events."

"And yet we have a guest from out of town who chose this hotel to stay at while attending the reunion. Not the Hawthorne. I don't want Hawthorne House to be the only venue handling this. I want to publicize that the Ocean Vista is a luxurious and competitive place to stay in Crystal Cove, so we get future contracts. Word travels. It'll open the door for other bigger contracts."

He *was* serious.

"Edward, I—"

"Violet Slyk will be filming a segment for the *Chart Toppers in Music* show on the beach in a few days for some guy named Sammy Fender who graduated with the class and is now a famous singer. I personally don't know who he is, but apparently, he's a big deal. Do you know him?"

"Um, yeah, Sean West. His stage name is Sammy Fender. I know you're still fairly new at the Ocean Vista, but you should know that I never ask for time off. And I get one vacation a year that I usually spend close to home so I can put out fires here," she said.

"So, you're not leaving town?"

"That's none of your business."

"I will take that as a no since you said you stick close to home. You can take time off the following two weeks."

"I chose this weekend to start my vacation."

His brow furrowed. He didn't know. He probably

didn't even look at the files. He relied on her too much, given that she'd been working at the Ocean Vista for the three years since she'd moved back to Crystal Cove and knew how the place ran. It wasn't in her job description as an event planner. She wasn't HR. She focused on weddings. She helped make memories for other people. She made their special events perfect. Or as perfect as she could make them despite the colors they chose.

And now she sounded like she was whining. A slow rise of irritation scraped its way up her spine as she realized how pathetic she sounded, even to her own ears. It shamed her that Edward was at least fifteen or twenty years younger than her, and she'd stooped this low just to make sure she wouldn't be anywhere near the class reunion this weekend.

"You didn't grow up here like I did, Edward. I didn't graduate from this class, but I know just about everyone coming to this reunion. And I…"

"All the more reason you should be here to welcome anyone who attends. You must know our guest."

Her stomach turned. "What is the person's name?"

"I don't remember. Someone from out of town."

"Obviously."

"I need a familiar face here, Meredith. I can't spare you. Carol and Louise are still too inexperienced to handle such a big event."

"What event? It's one guest!"

He ignored her. "Anything can go wrong. An opportunity could arise. I need you on-call all weekend when you aren't on a shift. My answer is no." His eyes held no sympathy or judging. This was business.

He relied on her to ensure that any opportunity to capitalize on this class reunion would come to the Ocean Vista.

"I'm not going to the reunion, Edward. I don't know what you expect of me."

"Keep your eyes and ears on alert. That's all."

Stifling the sigh making its way up her chest, she nodded.

Maybe Griffin wasn't coming to the reunion. He'd been career military for so long doing important work worldwide that maybe he didn't care about something as simple as a thirty-fifth high school reunion.

What was he these days? A Major? Colonel? After two tours as an enlisted airman, Griffin had commissioned to be an Officer and made a career out of the military without her.

The familiar irritation that she'd been keeping tabs on such things crept back into her mind, leaving her stomach sour. He hadn't returned to Crystal Cove in years, which strangely gave her a sense of comfort since she knew she wouldn't run into him on the street or in the supermarket and be caught off guard.

"Meredith!"

She sucked in a quick breath, wishing she'd been able to make it out the door and avoid Edward. Snapping her gaze back to Edward, she caught his scowl that was so strong her shoulders actually drooped enough for her to worry about dropping the tablecloths in her arms.

"You can't keep disappearing into the past like that. I need you to focus."

"It's a stupid high school reunion, Edward," she blurted out. "No one likes them except the geeks who go."

Ignoring her, he said, "I'm going to spread the word on social media that the Ocean Vista is an overflow hotel. Maybe we'll be able to piggyback on some free publicity with that Sammy Fender concert. I don't care about whatever high school tragedy has you on edge about this class reunion. And don't say you're not, because you've been jumping out of your skin for days."

She was about to protest, but he held up his hand.

"I'm sure whatever it is, everyone has forgotten about it by now. I need you here."

There weren't enough years for her to forget about Griffin Cole, and there weren't enough lifetimes. *Maybe he's not coming. Maybe he's staying at the main hotel and will never show his face here.* She could hope.

"That's easy for you to say. Have you even gone to any of your class reunions yet?"

"No. My twentieth is in two years, and I'm not going. Full stop."

It didn't surprise her. Edward tried to hand her the schedule for the reunion weekend. She could see the red pen notes he'd made. She glanced at the tablecloths in her arms when she didn't readily take it.

"I'll leave this on your desk."

She had a week to figure this out. Maybe she'd catch a forty-eight-hour flu and need to take some sick time. Edward would make her work, no doubt, but she'd threaten puking and any other nasties she could think of.

There were so many hotels and inns in Crystal Cove. What were the chances of Griffin Cole staying at *her* hotel if he came home for the reunion? There were rumors, and rumors had a way of growing legs. Maybe that's all they were. She probably had nothing to worry about, but that didn't squash the growing anxiety making its way up her throat.

A rush of warm air came racing into the automatic side door she'd just walked through, bathing her face and taking with it the anxiety that had her "on edge." Instinctively, Meredith lifted her face and breathed deeply as if she were on the beach and could feel the sun. But as she walked the concrete path on the side of the building, she was shaded by overgrown palm trees and greenery kept immaculate by the lawn company the hotel hired.

She needed a walk on the beach, not a day in heels with problems. The ocean was calling for her. She could hear the surf pounding into the shore. It was probably high tide, which she loved. She loved low tide for a different reason and at a different time of day. But she loved the power of high tide and how it left her sane and made her feel small, washing away the little things she obsessed over.

She'd make sure she got that walk on the beach in today. She needed to clear her head and forget about the rumors about Griffin Cole returning to Crystal Cove. She'd been unable to sleep for the past few weeks since she'd heard that little tidbit casually mentioned on social media. No one confirmed it, and she didn't want to ask. Talk about rumors. But if they were true, it would be a disaster.

"Well, this sucks."

Griffin Cole took a deep breath as he climbed out of the cab he'd taken from the Orlando airport and looked at the Ocean Vista Hotel's big letters outside the building above the revolving doors. Lucas actually managed to get him here.

He should have rented a car to make a quick getaway the moment he felt like…this. His stomach gurgled as whatever he'd munched on between the flight and the cab ride rolled around his stomach and protested. It was just nerves. The last time he'd stepped foot in Crystal

Cove, he'd proposed to Meredith Prichard, the woman he'd fallen head over heels with in high school. She'd sent him a Dear John letter a year later, breaking his heart.

Somewhere in this building, Meredith was sitting at a desk, unaware that he was about to step back into her life.

"The Ocean Vista is a popular hotel. People who stay here like it," the cab driver said, pulling his suitcase from the trunk of the cab.

Griffin handed the driver a tip and then grabbed the bag, dismissing the fact he'd heard the cab driver's words. "Thanks for the ride."

The cab driver smiled and nodded, pleased with the tip. "Any time. Call me if you need me."

He wasn't going to need him. When Griffin checked into the hotel, he would rent a car—no, a Jeep. Not a military-issue Jeep because he sat in those all the time. He'd get one with all the bells and whistles, a great stereo, and comfortable seats to drive along the coast and just chill. He had a lot of unwinding to do, and only music would get the job done.

His heart pounded as he stared at the circular drive and the bold letters on the hotel. The building was fairly new. It couldn't be more than twenty years old. It wasn't here when he'd lived in Crystal Cove.

He'd give anything to be back in Honolulu on his thirty-five-foot cruiser with Lucas just shooting the hay as they watched the sunset and talked about fishing. It had been Lucas's idea for him to come back to Crystal Cove. Griffin was a decorated Colonel in the Air Force, and he still managed to be talked into coming to his thirty-fifth high school reunion despite not stepping near this place in nearly as many years.

Crystal Cove hadn't been home for a very long time, as many places in the world had been over the years. But Hawaii was home now and probably would be until he died.

But at one time, Crystal Cove was his own slice of heaven, the only place that comforted him because Meredith Prichard lived here.

That is, until it didn't.

Bending down, he grabbed the suitcase the cab driver left on the hot pavement. Taking a moment to collect himself before taking steps into a past he had fought long and hard to forget and forgive, he forced his legs to move forward. With any luck, Meredith wouldn't even be here. He could be honest with Lucas and tell him he'd tried his best but failed. And then he would fly back to base and forget he ever agreed to confront Meredith Prichard.

Damn, when had he become such a wimp? And he was an Air Force Colonel, for God's sake.

"Man up, Cole."

The moment the air conditioning bathed his face as the revolving glass doors opened up into the lobby, he breathed a sigh of relief. A quick glance showed Meredith was nowhere to be found in the hotel lobby. His eyes grazed the open space beyond the lobby as he willed his heart to stop beating so fiercely. He didn't see her face nor hear that musical laugh, the same one that had haunted his dreams for years while he sat somewhere in the desert overseas.

He should have just stayed in another hotel. The Hawthorne House would be crawling with his classmates, trying to catch up on news, but what would be the point? He was here for Meredith. Yeah, he was curious about friends he knew when he was young. But it was her. He was keeping a promise.

Whatever happened, he'd live through it and then go back to his base where life didn't feel as surreal as it did right now in Crystal Cove, where the nerves flowing through his veins didn't make him want to jump out of his skin.

Slowly making his way across the polished marble floor lobby, he glanced around. Who was he kidding? He didn't care about the decor meant to be inviting to tourists and probably cost the owners a small fortune. He was searching for Meredith. For all he knew, she could be sitting in an occasion chair behind one of the many plants and palm trees they managed to squeeze into the lobby. She was probably holed up somewhere in the office where she ran, God knows what. He knew the military. He didn't know hospitality.

As he walked, he imagined there was a giant neon sign hovering above his head, letting everyone know how terrified he was to see his high school sweetheart again. And why? It had been over thirty years. They'd lived more time without each other than they'd lived together. They were strangers, really. The things that had drawn them together in their youths could have changed drastically. He'd changed. He wasn't the young man he used to be. It was only right that Meredith had changed, too.

If he kept telling himself that, maybe he'd actually believe it.

He reached the front desk, dropped his bag on the floor, and glanced at the young woman on the phone talking to a guest who was upset about the positioning of the beds and an extra cot from what he could make out quickly. As he waited for her to finish, he glanced around the lobby again. There was a seating area in the center with ample-sized upholstered chairs around a large round coffee table with an oversized centerpiece that made it impossible to comfortably see anyone who sat on the other side. Rather than ponder the purpose of it, he focused on a young couple who were being dragged through the lobby by their two school-aged children wearing bathing suits and floaties. He smiled as he realized they were probably headed for the beach or the hotel pool for some fun. The young couple wasn't much older than he and Meredith were the last time he'd seen her.

Taking a deep breath of the cool air as he turned back toward the woman behind the counter, he waited, staring at the ring bell sign next to a bell so he wouldn't stare at her as she tried her best to convince the guest on the phone that whatever was wrong in their room would be taken care of.

Maybe he still had enough time to make up a story about why he couldn't stay in Crystal Cove. Surely, there was a flight headed to the West Coast every hour or so that he could catch. From there, he could book a flight to Hawaii.

No. He'd given Lucas his word, and they'd shook hands on it. He deserved to have Griffin see this through.

His thoughts were interrupted by the phone being dropped into the cradle and a small sigh from the woman. When he turned to look at her, she'd already pasted on a smile.

After the phone conversation, the young woman appeared only slightly frazzled. She said, "I apologize for the delay. Do you have a reservation?"

The young woman was in her early twenties or maybe even late teens. Her name tag said Darcy, and he wondered if that was her first or last name. She looked at him with wide eyes and was eager to help. She'd be good in the military. She was focused and took the job seriously.

"No problem. I wasn't waiting long."

She cocked her head to one side. "You're being nice. I saw you while I was on the phone. I know you had to wait."

"Just a minute."

She started tapping on the computer screen and appeared to get frustrated when it wasn't working correctly. "It's going to be a busy weekend. I want to make sure I do a good job."

"Are you new here?"

She shook her head. "I just like to do the best I can. This computer is a bit…" Breathing a sigh of relief when it appeared her computer screen finally complied with her command, her shoulders eased, and she smiled. "Did you say you had a reservation?"

"Yes. Colonel Griffin Cole."

"Oh," she said with surprise after typing in his name. "You're here for the class reunion."

"Uh, yeah. How'd you know about that?"

"There is a annotation here in the computer."

"I thought all the events were happening at the Hawthorne House?"

"They are. But Mr. Mahoney has been talking about the old people's class reunion for days."

"Old people class reunion? Yeah, that would be me."

He stifled a chuckle that tickled his throat as her cheeks flamed with the realization of what she'd said aloud. She looked like a Darcy, if a name could fit a face, and she was mortified.

Punching a few more keys, her expression collapsed. She slowly lifted her gaze to him. "I'm so sorry. You're here for the…um…I'm really sorry. I shouldn't have repeated…"

He leaned into the registration counter. "It's okay. I won't tell anyone."

"Thank you. I'm really embarrassed." She clicked a few keys as she continued the process of registering him for his suite and taking his credit card and license. She glanced quickly at the license. "Colonel? That's like a big deal?"

He shrugged. "It's a big job."

"And you graduated from Crystal Cove High School?"

"A long time ago."

She reached for the printer, pulled out his receipt and then compiled his key and added a pamphlet with details about the resort. "I graduated from there, too. I haven't even gone to my fifth reunion yet, not that I want to. I can't imagine anyone I graduated with being a big shot."

"Is that what I am?"

"You're a Colonel. I've never met a Colonel before."

"Nice to meet you, Darcy."

She smiled and leaned closer to him with the counter between them, lowering her voice. "As soon as I have enough money saved, I'm out of here."

"You don't like Crystal Cove?"

She shrugged. "The beach. That's nice. But…" Her words trailed off as if just realizing she was confiding in a stranger. "It's nothing special."

"I hear you. There is a whole big world out there. So much to see. But sometimes coming home is special."

"Yeah. Okay." She shrugged uncomfortably and handed him a folder with his key card and information about the hotel. "It may be easier to go to your room by walking outside and following the path to the elevators on the other side of the resort. If you take the elevator in the lobby, you will have to walk through a maze of hallways to get to your room. That and at this time of the day, the main elevator is really crammed with people wanting to go to the pool."

"Thank you. And thanks for the tip."

He nodded as he turned and grabbed his luggage. He was right about one thing. The world was big and, in some ways, scary. But he didn't want to revisit memories of a time long past.

As he walked to the sliding doors he'd come through just a few minutes ago, he wondered when he'd gotten so jaded about home. Even though it seemed like a distant memory, Crystal Cove had been his home for many years. He had wonderful memories here. And one memory that pretty much rocked his world.

The familiar scent of the Atlantic Ocean filled his senses as he walked, giving Griffin a longing that brought to mind memories of high school and those years after when all that mattered to him was Meredith Prichard. Laughing and yelling from the beach and the pool area drowned out what he didn't want to think about as he walked the path along the hotel until he caught sight of a hammock tucked under a group of crossed palm trees in a secluded area.

Despite wanting to walk right past it, he paused and gripped the handle of his leather luggage tighter. There were hammocks all over the beach, tucked in hideaway dunes like this one up and down the beaches of Crystal Cove. During a thunderstorm, he and Meredith had made love one night in a hammock. They'd been convinced they'd be heard by the guests in a nearby hotel and laughed about how the thunder they felt was stronger than the thunder rolling into shore. They were wild, totally unabashed about their love for each other, and never cared who saw it. They just loved each other like no one else existed or mattered.

Back then, no one did.

A guttural sound made its way up his throat, accompanied by the over-thirty-year-old memory of touching Meredith in the hammock. They didn't have a blanket; they'd used whatever clothes they had to cover themselves when they'd bothered. It had been dark, and no one could see them tucked away under the palms. Yet, each lightning bolt illuminated her skin as it lit up the sky. Griffin felt himself growing hard just thinking of Meredith's smooth, warm skin pressed against his.

"Holy crap! It's you!"

And that voice only made his reaction worse as he turned and stood face to face with the woman and the memories he'd spent over thirty years trying to erase.

Griffin stared at the woman standing on the walkway holding a pile of white linens that looked like they were about to tumble from her arms. He'd chosen Ocean Vista because he'd discovered Meredith worked there. It would be easier to run into her here than at the class reunion hotel, where prying eyes were on them.

"You're a housemaid?"

She scowled, then lifted her chin. *Dead wrong words.*

"After all these years, *that* is the first thing you want to say to me?"

"It's better than 'holy crap.' Besides, you're the one holding towels. What am I supposed to think?"

Meredith drew a deep breath and glanced away, then back at him. He wasn't sure if it was because she was upset or just in a hurry and wanted to blow him off.

"Table linens," she said. "The staff put out the

wrong color on twenty tables. For some reason, the word purple escaped them. And what would it matter if I were a housemaid?"

"Purple tablecloths?"

"Don't start. I've already been through this. It wasn't my decision. I'm not the bride. And don't ignore the question."

He nodded, not missing the little wince from Meredith when she said *bride*. Were they talking about tablecloths, or was she thinking about their canceled wedding all those years ago? They hadn't laid eyes on each other in over thirty years. He'd thought about her just about every day, even though he'd tried his best to move on. The slightest thing that wasn't even remotely connected to her would somehow bring his mind back to Meredith.

They'd left so much unsaid. Since making the decision to come back to Crystal Cove, he'd rehearsed this moment a hundred times, but he was clueless about where to begin.

"I'm getting the feeling you're not happy to see me, Meredith."

"You're kidding, right?"

"Why would I joke about something like this?"

Her mouth dropped open and then quickly shut.

"I didn't think I'd see you. I didn't think you'd come to the reunion."

"I never thought I'd see you again."

"Well, the way things ended—"

"There was an end? You stopped writing. Well, except for that *one* letter."

"You stopped calling. That is, when you called at all. I got a call once a month."

"You called off our wedding!"

"Let's not go there."

"Why not? We didn't go there when it mattered."

"I can't…"

Her voice trailed off, and her eyes widened when she saw the place that had paralyzed him. He knew immediately where she'd gone.

Breathless, she said, "It was a long time ago. I don't have time to talk. I…I have to go."

As she breezed by him, he caught a whiff of her perfume. No, not perfume. She never liked to spray perfume on herself, at least not thirty years ago. Most likely, it was her favorite lotion. She loved lotions, and *he'd like rubbing it on her body.*

He hadn't thought about that in years, and there it was popping into his brain in a collection of other memories now flooding his mind.

"Really? Already?"

HE ACTUALLY HAD THE NERVE TO LOOK UPSET. Meredith didn't want Griffin to look upset. She was upset. She had feared this very moment for so long. It was her turn to be upset.

"I'm working, Griffin, not on vacation."

"Meredith."

She turned on her heels to look at him again. *Big mistake.* Once was enough to rattle her to the core.

Damn him. He was as handsome and slender as he was at twenty before he'd left for boot camp. His broad shoulders had filled in considerably. They had during those first years of Air Force training. His button-down shirt stretched against chest muscles that were still as inviting as they were when she ran her hand over his skin. Meredith didn't have to touch them to know how they felt. She could feel it now against her fingers. *Her body remembered.*

"You have some nerve to come here and be so handsome after all this time."

And then he smiled that smile that used to melt her

heart, and she realized she'd spoken her thoughts aloud. He was the one man she truly felt comfortable doing that with. But suddenly, she felt as if the heels of her shoes were melting into the concrete beneath her, and her cheeks flamed. Her head was swimming, and her body was so off-kilter that the weight of the tablecloths had her bending forward as she fought to keep herself upright.

"You still think I'm handsome, huh?"

"You wish."

"You just said it."

"Oh, never mind!"

If she had a shred of dignity left, she'd abandon it and run, tossing the tablecloths aside on the flowers lining the path. But she held tight.

"Where are you going?"

"Laundry."

His low chuckle at her back sent a fingernail of irritation up her spine. She was fully aware that her reaction to seeing Griffin again had irritated her, not that in a matter of thirty seconds he'd been able to make her heart race and her body sweat just by looking at him.

It was official. *She hated Edward.* And she was going to tell him so.

WITH A SMILE STILL ON HIS FACE, GRIFFIN COULDN'T keep his eyes off Meredith until she disappeared into a side door. Only then did he turn back to the path and walk in the opposite direction toward the elevators Darcy mentioned.

"That went better than I expected," he said to himself. *Lucas would be proud.*

Griffin had showered, shaved, and changed into a comfortable pair of jeans and his favorite T-shirt an hour later. A quick call to a local car rental company ended in disappointment since he couldn't get a Jeep until the following day. That meant he was stuck at the hotel for dinner or any place that was within walking distance unless he took a cab. He didn't relish the idea of dealing with a cab to and from wherever he ended up, so he decided to take a walk.

Once down in the lobby, now filled with people dressed to the nines, most likely for the event with the purple tablecloths Meredith mentioned, he made his way through the crowd to the registration desk and asked about some local eateries. Some of his classmates coming in for the reunion were already in town and staying at the Hawthorne House. He wasn't ready to venture into small talk when the reunion festivities hadn't formally begun.

And who was he kidding? Running into Meredith again would be a major plus if he stuck nearby, which surprised even him.

"Still here?" he said to Darcy who was looking a bit more tired than she was earlier. But she still pasted a smile on her face.

"Leaving in about ten minutes," she said. "How can I help you?"

"What's the best place on the beach to get a burger?"

"Our hotel restaurant has good food. You should try it."

"I was thinking of taking a walk. I'm guessing a lot of the places I used to go when I was last here are no longer in business."

"Tanks is still on the main strip along the beach.

They must have burgers. My parents said they used to go there when we first moved here."

It dawned on him that Darcy may very well be the daughter of someone he'd gone to school with. "When was that?"

"I was three. I don't ever remember living anywhere else, but I guess we used to live in Georgia."

"Your parents like Tanks?"

"Every Friday night."

"Well, that's saying something."

"They're old. They're in their forties."

His eyes widened and her expression collapsed. "Is that so? Thank you for the recommendation."

He didn't remember Tanks from when he was last here. It was probably named something else when he was in high school.

He stepped outside, and the late afternoon heat slapped him in the face. It had been a long time since the humidity of Florida hit him so hard. The trade winds off the water around Oahu were much more pleasing than summer in Florida, and he wasn't used to it anymore. But as soon as he walked past the hotel, the cool breeze coming off the Atlantic Ocean bathed him, making him forget the discomfort.

Ever since this afternoon, Griffin couldn't shake the jumbled emotions distracting him. He knew coming home wasn't going to be easy. He'd expected the first time he laid eyes on Meredith again; his anger would surface. He'd been so upset when he'd gotten her letter breaking off the wedding. And then years later...even the thought of confronting Meredith then had made his blood boil. His career in the military had been a good excuse not to process why a love like theirs was suddenly over. They'd promised to have a life together. They never needed a marriage certificate to be committed. Or so he thought. He'd counted on their love. Then it was gone.

He shook his head as he walked down the main strip along the beach. For all he knew, he'd passed half a dozen of his former classmates, and he didn't even recognize them. He wasn't looking at any of the people. The crowd around him was just blank faces, much like the empty shell he suddenly felt growing around him.

Griffin knew Meredith's face. He knew the quick hitch of her breath when she was excited. She'd tried to dismiss him earlier when he'd surprised her on the path at the hotel. But her reaction to him said it all.

He approached a small shack that smelled amazing. The fried food on the dishes of people walking away from the window and settling on the picnic tables out front made his mouth water. Griffin never minded eating alone. He'd had many stiff dinner meetings dressed in his uniform and uncomfortable lunches with administrators that upset his stomach. He wasn't a stranger to confrontation. But he didn't relish hashing things out with Meredith. And he would before he left Crystal Cove. He had to.

But not tonight. Tonight, he needed to get rid of this crazy, unsettled feeling he had to kiss Meredith again. Somehow, he'd convinced himself that she wouldn't rattle him, that he wouldn't long to touch her after just a few moments together.

Damn, he was a fool.

There was always something about the color of her deep-blue eyes that reminded him of the ocean. They were still as blue as ever. He recalled how her cheeks were always slightly burned from being in the sun, no matter how much she tanned or put on sunscreen. That hadn't changed. She used to laugh and say her skin would be leather by the time she was fifty. But in those few seconds on the path, he'd longed to brush his fingers over her sun-kissed cheek.

What shocked him the most was that his anger toward her for so many years had vanished instantly. It was still there, buried deep inside him somewhere, and it would rear its ugly head in time. It was easy to remember the rage while he walked along the strip with a container of burgers and fries, but not when she'd been standing right in front of him.

He drank his cold soda on the way back to the hotel. If he got hungry later, he'd eat the food. With any luck, he wouldn't run into Meredith again tonight even though he lied to himself about wanting to. He just didn't have enough energy for confrontations tonight.

"ONE GUEST, EDWARD. I SHOULDN'T BE HELD HOSTAGE the entire week for one guest. There are no more events until Sunday, and Maureen has that one covered. It's easy."

Edward sat at his desk and folded his hands on some paperwork. "How did the purple wedding go?"

"Perfect. Everything went off without a hitch."

"Exactly the reason I need you here."

Exasperated, she threw out her arms and let them fall to her side. Exhaustion was beating her down physically and emotionally. She didn't want to be standing there anymore. The rest of the day staff were heading home soon, and she wanted to be going with them, not ducking corners trying to stay invisible.

"I'm going home, Edward. There's nothing for me to do here for the rest of the week. Maureen has my number if she has any questions about the event on Sunday."

"That's not true. I could use your help with these financial reports."

"I'm not admin. I'm events. I already submitted my reports."

"I thought you were a team player."

"I am. With my team. I'm not going to step in and do your job, Edward. I'm going home."

"Meredith?"

"I'm leaving! I'll be back in the morning to check on things, but I am not staying the whole day."

She barely heard his voice as she walked out of his office and headed down the hall to the lobby so she could slip out the door.

She was just about to make her escape through the revolving door when she heard, "Meredith?"

It wasn't Edward, but she needed a quick getaway before she ran into Griffin.

"Darcy, I'm not supposed to be here."

She turned and found Darcy with her hand perpendicular to her face, hiding her other hand pointing to the lobby chairs.

"The Colonel's been waiting a while," she whispered. "He's cute."

"No, he's not," she lied.

Darcy's shoulders darted up as she giggled. "You're such a liar."

Dragging in a quick breath, she made her way over to Griffin, who was stretched out in the sofa chair as if about to fall asleep.

"I'm working, Griffin. I'm sorry. I don't have time to visit."

He snapped his gaze to her and then stood up. "I thought maybe we could have dinner?"

"No."

His shoulders sagged only slightly, but she heard the defeat in his voice. "Meredith, we really need to talk. Don't you think?"

"No. Look, I'm happy you're doing well. I'm doing well. We're good. We don't have to talk about anything. *We* were a long time ago. There's nothing to talk about."

As she walked away, she sidestepped a luggage rack full of bags and a guest pushing the cart. But Griffin got caught waiting for the luggage rack and the party who owned it to pass.

She made the mistake of turning around long enough to let Griffin catch up to her. "Why aren't you at the reunion? Isn't that the reason you came to Crystal Cove?"

"Well, that's not the only reason. The reunion doesn't officially start until tomorrow. There's a cocktail party tomorrow night if you want to go."

"Why would I want to do that? It's not my graduating class. It's yours."

"But you know just about everyone in that class. We all did. Crystal Cove High School wasn't huge."

"It's not a good idea."

"Why not?"

She searched for words that wouldn't make her sound petty but came up empty.

"We have too much history, Griffin."

"All the more reason we should catch up."

"It's not a good idea."

"Why not?"

She sighed and looked away for a moment. "I think you should go to the cocktail party yourself. Besides, my boss is ready to chain me to my desk to keep me here. I was supposed to be on vacation right now, but he pulled my request at the last second."

"What for?"

"Apparently, you."

His brow furrowed.

"It doesn't matter," she said. "Edward will chain me to my desk if I don't leave here now. Have a good night, Griffin."

"Did you ever love me?"

The air sucked out of her lungs in an instant.

"What?"

"You heard me."

"I can't do this now. Maybe, being a Colonel, you can extract whatever information you want from people, but not from me. Don't talk to me."

GRIFFIN WATCHED MEREDITH STOMP OUT OF THE hotel through the revolving doors. He'd been out of line. Yes, he'd need to ask. It was only one of many questions he needed to talk to her about. But not in the lobby of a hotel with tourists milling about.

The cell phone in his pocket vibrated. He could only hear the soft ring when he pulled it out and held it in his hand. Glancing down at the caller ID, he hit the green button.

"That didn't take long, Lucas. I thought you were going to wait to call me on Friday."

"Did you talk to her?"

"Meredith is working. It's been hard to make the time."

"She can't work twenty-four-seven. But you saw her, right?"

"I did."

"And?"

He headed down to the center of the lobby. "There is no *and* other than saying hello and small talk for a few minutes. We haven't had time to talk."

"You've lost your mojo, Griff."

Griffin laughed. "I may have a few years on me, but my mojo is still intact. I still have moves."

"I've heard your knees crack when you walk. You can barely run these days. I'm surprised you aren't using a walker yet. I wouldn't rely so heavily on your moves, old man," Lucas said, laughing.

"Are you challenging me to another race?"

"I'm not going to take advantage of the elderly."

Griffin scoffed. "You just wait until I get back to Hawaii."

"Ooo, I'm scared."

He laughed. "I'll call you tomorrow."

He hung up the phone feeling significantly better than he did when he watched Meredith walk out of the building. Lucas was not going to hold out forever.

CHAPTER 3

"*Y*ou're talking to me?"

Once again, Griffin had stalked the lobby, waiting for Meredith. Lucas was right. He'd lost his mojo. He was pathetic.

"That depends on what you consider talking." She gave him a sidelong glance as she stood by the registration desk, waiting to talk to Darcy, who was again on the phone. "If you need something, Raymond is at the Concierge desk. He knows everything about everything."

"Does he know your work schedule?"

She turned toward him now. "Excuse me?"

"Are you working tomorrow…tonight? Today even?"

"I'm here, aren't I?"

He glanced down at her clothes. Unlike yesterday when she'd worn a dress and heels, Meredith had chosen a pair of jeans and a nice T-shirt that she tucked into her waist. She had flat sandals on her feet. He didn't have to say anything. Her expression said it all.

"I'm only here for a few hours this morning. Why does it matter what my schedule is?"

"Humor me."

"Why would I do that?"

"Because I have plans."

Her mouth dropped open, and it occurred to him how his words sounded.

"Good for you."

"With you."

"Is that right?"

"Yes. I intend to spend as much time as possible with you, Meredith."

She shook her head in disbelief. "Why?"

"Because we have unfinished business. You know it's true. And I'm your one guest."

"Excuse me?"

"Darcy told me there was only one guest staying here attending the class reunion, and your boss wants me to be taken care of. I think that's how she said it. Some annotation in the computer or something? So, are you free today? If you tell me, you'll save me the trouble of walking across the lobby to visit Raymond, who I believe isn't at his desk because of some crisis one of the staff is having regarding a guest not getting his food delivery service, even though it's not from the hotel. I heard them both complaining as they walked away. If you tell me what your schedule is for the next few days, it'll save me having to wait for him to come back only to then come back and ask you because I have a feeling he'd send me to you anyway."

"Griffin, stop."

"Come on. Humor me."

"Are you asking me on a date?"

"I am. To the karaoke mixer tomorrow night."

She sputtered. "You call that a date?"

"Give me a break. You love karaoke." At her reaction, he added, "You don't wanna go and see a bunch of us make fools of ourselves by singing old '80s music no one listens to anymore?"

She lifted a finger. "The hell they don't. The '80s are still my jam. Always were. Always will be."

"I remember," he laughed.

"There you go, making fun again and sweet-talking me using '80s music as a bribe."

"Does that mean you'll go? It'll be a good time. As spectators, anyway. Since I moved up the ranks, I don't get to let my hair down very much anymore."

"What hair?"

"It's not like high school. But it's longer than the standard military buzz cut. I actually miss the long hair."

"You're too…"

"Old?"

Meredith shrugged, moving a few steps aside when someone approached the desk to check out. "I didn't say that."

He nodded. "But you were going to. You know, I can do math. You hit the big 'five oh' recently, too."

"Sticks and stones. Besides, that's yesterday's news. Fifty is the new thirty-five."

"Is that right?" He reached up and scratched what little hair he had and watched her try her best to stifle a laugh. She still did that little shift of the jaw to keep herself from showing she thought what he said was funny.

There was a time when he could make her laugh. He missed that laugh. He hadn't thought much about it. His intention was to talk with her, hash things out, and keep his promise. But now, his mission was to get Meredith to laugh. A lot.

"With such a busy schedule, I would have assumed you gave up your singing days years ago."

"Why would you think that?"

Shrugging, she said, "You're a Colonel. That's serious business."

"It is. But I'm not a stick in the mud. I still do the occasional concert in the shower. Sean West isn't the only musical talent in our class. Come on. It will be fun. You used to be quite the singer in high school."

She sputtered. "In the choir? I think that hardly qualifies me to sing karaoke in a public place where everyone has a smartphone to record my humiliation."

"No one is qualified for karaoke. That's the point. We all stink at it. But it's fun."

If anyone else were asking, Griffin knew Meredith would have actually looked forward to it. She would have jumped at the chance. But he was asking. What did she say to him last night? They had too much history. And not enough of what should have happened in between their history and today. His mission had changed. And he never failed.

MEREDITH PULLED HER SUNGLASSES DOWN TO THE bump in her nose and took in the vehicle in front of her. Griffin gave her a goofy smile that reminded her of when he was twenty years old, the last time she'd seen him drive an open Jeep.

"This is a bad idea," she said. "I can't believe I let you talk me into spending the day together."

His expression faltered only slightly. "What do you mean?"

"Remember the last time we drove in an open SUV? It was a death trap."

"You're talking about my first car?"

"Is that what you are calling it? It was a death trap. As I recall, you and Tyler Conner put together a bunch of parts from different cars you got for next to nothing from a junkyard to make…something street-worthy."

He chuckled. "It was just enough to make it legal. I loved that car. I wish I still had it."

"I don't even know what kind of car that was."

"A little bit of everything, really. But hey, this is a brand-new Jeep."

She cocked her head to one side. "The wheels fell off."

"Only one. We fixed it. Did you hear me? This is practically a brand-new vehicle. I think it has seven thousand miles on it. Practically a baby."

"I heard you. It has no doors."

"Live on the edge. It'll be fun."

She cocked her head to one side. "Where are we going with this?"

"The beach," they both said. She knew.

Then he added, "Maybe a ride up to Jacksonville if you're up for it."

"Jacksonville, huh?"

He came around the front of the Jeep and stopped at the passenger without a door. "This one is pretty, huh?"

She couldn't disagree. It was definitely cool. "Red. I like the color. At least the wheels won't fall off this one."

She climbed in and settled in the smooth leather seats as her head swam with doubt.

"You aren't trying to recreate old memories, are you?"

"You wound me," he said, climbing into the driver's seat.

"Impossible."

"I've been in the trainwreck before."

"I'm a trainwreck?"

"You made *me* a trainwreck. There is a difference, and I only recently realized this."

"Wow. And that's all on me, huh? I'm not the one who decided to reenlist months before our wedding."

"Well…point taken. I may have been a little impulsive."

"It doesn't take much if memory serves."

"It does. I may have taken for granted you'd be okay with my decision."

"That's for sure."

"In my defense, you've always knocked me off my feet with a single look. If I'd been able to see your face instead of waiting weeks for a letter, I would have known better."

She smiled instinctively at the compliment. She still had an effect on him. Why she should care, she didn't know. But after a few seconds, it didn't feel good.

"How does my knocking you off your feet have anything to do with this?"

"It doesn't. It was my mistake. I'm sorry."

"Well, it's water under the bridge now. We can't change the decisions we made back then."

"Maybe not. But I am sorry I took you for granted if that means anything. The more time I spend here, the more I realize things would have been different for us if I hadn't."

"We said we weren't going to talk about us."

He glanced at her quickly as he drove. His hand was resting on the wheel and his shoulders were eased back into the seat as if he hadn't a care in the world. She remembered him like this. There were so many memories of them like this. Why had she let him talk her into spending the day together? They'd agreed that they wouldn't talk about their breakup. They would just fill in the pieces of their lives that they missed. But it was becoming apparent that doing so was impossible.

She was quiet for a moment and then needed to know. "You really think we would have had a shot at staying together if you had told me?"

He gazed at her with more maturity but with the same intensity of the young man he'd been when they'd fallen in love. "I do. Don't you?"

Damn. As he took the turn that would bring them along the coastal road, Meredith turned memories and letters around in her mind. They were words. Old and tired now. They'd lived a lifetime without each other, yet this was so familiar. It was as if yesterday was thirty years ago, and Griffin was on leave. They were riding to the coast and talking about their wedding plans.

And the simple words Griffin said, "I do" made her question every decision and every moment of her life since.

It had taken Meredith years to move on from Griffin Cole. It was the very reason she'd asked, no begged, Edward to approve her vacation time so she could avoid feeling all these emotions she knew would come rushing back and want her to crawl into a hole and hide. Griffin hadn't stepped foot in Crystal Cove in years, making it easier for her to pretend she was over him and what had happened between them. Now, he was sitting tall in his seat, looking as gorgeous as he was in his youth and making her heart race with just a single look.

Damn, why had she agreed?

He just walked into her life again as if he'd never left. Except it wasn't the same. He didn't love her like he had. He wouldn't reach across the seat and touch her in his playful way as he did when they were together. He wasn't going to pull her into his arms and make love to her either.

She knew it would be difficult. She knew there were skeletons that needed to come out, and they terrified her. But Meredith hadn't expected to still be in love with him. Or that he could still stop her heart from beating with a single smile.

And he could. He did. And she was toast.

The familiar ache in her heart grew. No one wanted regrets, and she had so many. She wasn't going to survive Griffin Cole again. And there was no way to stop her fall. Not now. A small part of her wanted to just go with it and give herself one last time to be with Griffin and know that passion and excitement before he returned to his base. She could do that, couldn't she?

"I don't have a cat," she finally said.

He glanced at her; his eyebrows furrowed. "Um, neither do I."

"You probably have a dog."

"Did. Buster. He died about a year ago."

"I'm sorry."

"Thank you. Why are we talking about cats and dogs?"

She shifted uncomfortably in the bucket seat and felt the pothole they'd just run over more intensely than she probably should.

"I live alone. But I don't want you to think I'm a cat lady who goes to work and then has a million cats she lives with."

His smile was slow. "A million would be bad. One or two isn't a crisis."

"No. But people always assume that if you're an unmarried woman in your fifties living alone, you must have half a dozen cats because you're lonely. I'm not lonely. My life is full. I do things."

"Things are good."

"Yes. I have friends. I travel. I'm not a cat lady."

"Okay, you're not a cat lady. Just for the record, I wouldn't mind if you had a cat. I kinda like them."

"Yeah? Since when?"

"I know people with cats."

"Women?"

He chuckled, and she hated him for it. "Some."

She rubbed a spot on her chest that was hidden by her shirt, then stared at him for a moment as they drove. "This is a stupid conversation, isn't it?"

"You started it."

"I know."

Years. She was feeling them all now. There were so many things about being with Griffin that transported her back to the time when she wouldn't leave the house without making sure she had her pastel crop top and acid-washed jeans on. Griffin loved them. Or so he said. He would watch her walk ahead of him. She'd turn around and see the grin on his face, and she knew what he was thinking about. Yesterday wasn't so distant. Not in her mind, anyway. It felt as close as the distance between the seats of the Jeep right now. She could touch them as easily as she could reach out and touch Griffin if she tried.

It was the time between that felt otherworldly to her. There was so much of it. She wasn't wearing her pastel crop top or her acid-wash jeans. She wore dressier jeans to work because her comfortable go-to jeans, which she liked to wear on beach walks, were threadbare in places and not fit for the office. Her behind wasn't what it once was, but she didn't look so bad for a woman of fifty-one.

"You have a tattoo," he finally said, cutting into his thoughts. "What is it?"

"How do you know that?"

"When you were walking on the path with all those tablecloths in your arms, they pulled at your shirt, and I saw just a hint of one on your chest. I couldn't see what it was."

She drew in a deep breath. It was too soon. They weren't there yet. They'd gone from talking about death-trap vehicles to cats. "It's private."

To her relief, he let it go.

"How about you?"

"What about me?" Playing ignorant wasn't exactly her thing. She'd learned to be direct in a world with so many false messages. It was a good trait for her job. But it surprised Meredith that she'd resorted to old ways with Griffin.

"We have a long drive ahead of us. Jacksonville is at least two hours from Crystal Cove."

She glanced at the road ahead and then back at Griffin. "Jacksonville? Are you taking me to Dames Point Park?"

"Do you mind?" he asked. "We don't have to go if you don't want to."

"No, it's fine. You didn't want to do any of the events with the class?"

He shook his head. "I'm not much of a golfer unless I have to play with other military officers. The dolphin cruise was a hard pass. I don't want to be stuck on a boat unless it's mine."

"And you can make a quick getaway?"

He chuckled. "Right. And I don't drink tea."

"Tea?"

"There is a tea get-together."

"Oh. Yeah, you don't seem the tea type. Karaoke is more your speed."

"Exactly. Have you ever been?"

"To karaoke? Of course."

"Dames Point Park. The memorial."

"No. I just…no."

He looked out at the road ahead for a moment and then sighed. "The memorial for classmates who have passed isn't until tomorrow. I'm not sure I'll go. Maybe I'll go. It's always sad to learn someone from childhood has passed."

"I know."

"Have you been to Dames Point Park?"

"No. I haven't since I've returned to the East Coast. The *El Faro* went down while I was still in Ohio."

She shifted uncomfortably in her seat and watched the scenery momentarily, taking in the beauty of the coastal road. "Marie…she was your friend, really. She was always nice to me, but we weren't close. I guess I felt like I was intruding. I didn't realize you'd heard about what happened."

"Why wouldn't I? I may not have been back to Crystal Cove in years, but word travels far. She was a sailor. She loved the sea. She was…"

"Your best friend."

He shook his head and looked at her. The intensity of his expression hit her square in the chest. "You were my best friend. She knew that."

She didn't know why, but Griffin's admission

suddenly meant the world to her, even after all these years.

"But Marie was special," she said.

"She was a dear friend. We had known each other since kindergarten. We were close. She understood me."

"The way I didn't."

He shook his head. "We were a lot alike. Our passions. She worked doing what she loved. The sea, the open air, being on a ship out in the ocean—that was her passion. The few letters I got from her over the years let me know she was happy doing what she did. Do you mind going with me?"

"Why would I?"

"You won't be…"

"Jealous?" Meredith chuckled. Suddenly overcome with emotion, she turned away and felt the wind from the ride whip her hair around her face. "No. I'm not the same young girl who got up in arms about every turn of your head. At least, I'd like to think so. Besides, what would be the point of being jealous now?"

"Thank you."

The calm that crossed his expression as he drove was real. Meredith couldn't think of a time when she'd ever felt closer to Griffin.

CHAPTER 4

*L*ess than two hours later, they arrived in Jacksonville and headed down the narrow road to the tip of Dames Point Park, assumed to be the last point of United States soil the *El Faro* crew saw during their last voyage before the ship sank. The emotion that draped over Meredith like a cloud belied the beautiful day. The sun shone on the white caps of the water like diamonds. As she stepped out of the Jeep, the breeze flowed over her but did nothing to relieve her heavy heart.

This wasn't going to be easy for either of them, but it would be hardest on Griffin.

The wind swept through her hair, which she pushed away so she could turn and look at Griffin's reaction. And when she did, his expression broke her heart. It had been years since Marie had died along with the crew of the *El Faro*. But Griffin's expression was so raw it was as if Marie had just died.

"Do you still want to do this?" she asked.

"Of course. We've come this far."

"I can stay in the Jeep if you'd rather do this alone."

"I want you with me."

She drew a slow breath and tried not to read anything more into his words. Instead, she let him lead her down the path toward the monument that had been erected in memorial of the *El Faro* crew.

When they reached the memorial, Griffin paused before running his hand down the list of names on the memorial stone until he came to Marie's. He was silent as he tapped her name with his fingers. Meredith stayed back. She hadn't been close to Marie, but she knew Griffin had known her practically from the cradle. Marie had been a free spirit and a shining light for the Class of 1989. Even though they were coming to the memorial for the first time, other class members had visited or paid homage to Marie in their own way. Marie will be remembered tomorrow when they have the class memorial for lost classmates.

He glanced down at his phone and started searching.

Confused, she asked, "What are you doing?"

"Looking through my playlist of songs by The Who."

She chuckled. "Her favorite band."

He smiled as he glanced up at her. "It's fitting." He finished what he'd started and then set the phone in front of the memorial as the music to *Another Tricky Day* started playing.

"You know we have to dance it out now," Meredith said as she started to move to the opening guitar riff.

"Of course. Marie would. And she wouldn't give a damn who saw her doing it."

The opening instrumental had Griffin imitating Pete Townsend playing air guitar, and suddenly, Meredith was transported back to a time when neither of them had a care in the world.

In an instant she hadn't expected, Griffin hooked his arm around her waist and pulled her close, lifting her off her feet and spinning her as the music played. She threw her head back and laughed until tears filled her eyes. When her feet touched the ground again, he held onto her, gazing down into her eyes and moving closer before letting her go and spinning himself as the music played. Still feeling weightless from being in his arms, they held each other's hands, danced, and jumped as one in a ridiculously fun way, ignoring the occasional passing boat in the bay as the song played.

As the song began to wind down, Griffin pulled her into his arms again and held her close, stealing her breath away. His face was just inches from hers. As she gazed into his eyes, she felt his breath against her cheek and marveled at how much she wanted him to kiss her. She did nothing to prevent it. She held on to his shoulders and kept her gaze steady on him, allowing herself the luxury of feeling they were the only two people in the world at that moment, as she had done many times in her youth.

She was only vaguely aware of the increasing sound of wheels on the concrete path coming closer. Only then did each of them turn their heads to find two skateboarders on the path racing toward them.

"Hey, grandpa! Looking good!" one of them said.

The other added, "Keep at it. Totally drip song!"

"Drip? Who are you calling 'grandpa?'" he called out. The two young men stopped before them as the music died to nothing.

"Hey, no problem, pop. It's all cool. You both can groove pretty good at your age."

Griffin scrutinized the two young men and wanted to stare them right into the pavement for interrupting the moment he'd almost kissed Meredith. *Almost.* And it hurt like hell he didn't get to partake in that pleasure after the dance they'd just shared and hearing Meredith's musical laugh above the sound of The Who, Marie's favorite band.

But now Meredith was out of his arms and had stepped back.

The two men, who had short, cropped hair and dog tags hanging out of their T-shirts, were now sweaty and gross from skateboarding in the baking sun.

"Both of you are military." It wasn't a question. Griffin already knew. He met at least a dozen new recruits just like these two every week.

The shorter one flipped his skateboard by stepping on the back of the board until it spun. He then caught it with his hand and smiled, apparently proud of his skill.

"Good catch," Griffin said.

"Just came home on leave from the Air Force Academy. My buddy has never been to Florida, so I took him home for the sites."

"I see. Second-Class Cadet? Third-Class Cadet?"

"First-Class Cadet. You know your stuff, grandpa."

"Yeah, let's dispel with the 'grandpa,' shall we? How about Colonel Griffin Cole, USAF, Pearl Harbor-Hicham."

The blood drained instantly from the kids' faces. Meredith stifled a chuckle as she turned away for a second, unable to hide her laughter. Part of Griffin wanted her to throw her head back and laugh as she'd done when he spun her in his arms a few minutes ago.

The young men instantly straightened their backs and looked ahead as if in formation.

"Skateboards in front of a monument honoring fallen sailors? Really?" Griffin said in admonishment.

"I'm sorry, Colonel," the taller kid said with sudden respect. "I meant no disrespect."

"Save that for your CO. I'm not sure he'll be thrilled to get a call from me telling him what just went down. It's fine to get some R&R, but I suggest you think about where you are at all times, and who you're addressing."

"Yes, sir."

"On your way."

Meredith bit her lip to keep from laughing again. Oh, what he wouldn't do to tug on her sweet lips and kiss her. The shorter one made the mistake of dropping the skateboard on the ground as if he were about to skate off again. He thought better of it, picked it up, and tucked it under his arm.

As they disappeared down the path toward the bridge, walking quickly but not skateboarding, Meredith turned to Griffin. "Did you really just pull rank for fun?"

"They don't know that. I thought the taller one was going to wet himself." He shook his head. "Was I ever that boneheaded?"

"Yes."

"Thanks a lot."

"We all were. It was the '80s."

Griffin bent down to pick up his phone. Then, glanced in the direction the young airmen disappeared in. "Grandpa? Do I really look that old?"

She couldn't help but laugh. "Quit your complaining. Lots of our classmates are already grandparents, so yeah. That's us. Even if we don't have grandkids."

Giving her a mischievous grin, he continued to dance toward her. "Grandpas still got the moves. I can rock-n-roll with the best of them."

He reached for her, but she turned at the last second and started walking away from the monument.

"We should be getting back," she said.

"How about lunch first?"

"If we get it to go. I need to get back to my office."

Eating in the Jeep while Griffin drove proved challenging. But at least it gave them something to do other than talk. Eating wasn't enough to fill up time or keep Meredith from thinking about being in Griffin's arms.

He'd been ready to kiss her. And she would have let him. Hell, she would have been right in there with him. He wasn't going to have to try hard. But then the skateboarders ruined everything.

Or maybe not. Giving in to how they felt in the moment may have been the worst thing both of them could do. Maybe they dodged a bullet.

All this morning, on the ride to Dames Point Park, she'd been happy. She wasn't running away from Griffin. They were together, and it felt good. Maybe it was time to move on from the past.

ALL IT TOOK WAS DANCING TO AN '80S SONG FOR Griffin to get her in his arms again and make Meredith melt like chocolate in the hot sun. It was impossible for her to see herself as the fifty-plus woman who'd put herself through college and made a life for herself. She could take care of herself now, unlike the young girl who'd been a puddle on the floor when she'd sent Griffin that letter that ended everything. Griffin's voice cut into her thoughts.

"Did you ever marry? Did you ever love someone after me?"

Meredith drew a deep breath and gazed at the length of the road ahead, hoping to stretch out that answer. It shouldn't matter. But for some reason, how she would answer felt like a betrayal.

"I did."

Silence. When she couldn't stand it anymore, she continued,

"Rafe and I were married for eight years, but we lived together as man and wife for nearly four. The divorce dragged on simply because neither of us wanted to admit we'd made a mistake." She shook her head. "I knew better, but I married him anyway."

He glanced at her quickly and then turned his attention to the road. "You didn't love him?"

She shrugged. "There was love. There was kindness. There was nothing wrong with us on the outside. But it took a long time to realize it wasn't working."

It was hard to talk to Griffin about a relationship that was so long ago and was a failure. There was nothing wrong with Rafe and her. But there was. It wasn't what love was supposed to be. *It wasn't what she had with Griffin.*

"There wasn't much on the inside to keep us together, as much as we wanted there to be. We tried," she said so quietly she could barely hear her voice above the sound of the Jeep's tires rolling over the hot tar. It shamed her to say it, but she'd been relieved when the divorce was finalized.

"Why did you marry him?"

"Does it matter?"

He shrugged and then shook his head slowly. "I guess not."

Closing her eyes briefly, she steeled herself. "We'd dated for about six months before Rafe got a job offer he couldn't turn down in Ohio. Mom had been living in

Arizona for a while and my brother was in New York. I stayed after they left but…there really wasn't much for me in Crystal Cove anymore. He asked me to marry him. He wanted me to go to Ohio with him and build a life. He asked. He said he wouldn't go if it meant losing me. I said yes. I can't really explain it."

"You just did." Griffin glanced at her. "He asked."

What hung in the air was the real divide. Griffin never asked how she felt about him reenlisting. He just signed on for four more years of being in the Air Force, living his life in a war zone and expecting her to wait until he was ready for her.

Meredith peered at him as he drove, hoping he'd look at her so she could read his expression. But she didn't have to see his face straight-on to note the regret etched on his face. Damn, she hated regret.

"He was a good man, Griffin. We just jumped into it and then stayed together too long. It all made sense in the moment, and then the moment was gone, and we both were left to wonder why we were even together at all."

"Children?"

She shook her head. The thought of it made her stomachache and her heart hurt. "My best years were spent trying to make that marriage work and convince myself that if only I tried harder. It's been years since the divorce. But he still calls and checks in with me. He's married now and has a family. I'm happy for him."

He frowned. "You still stay in touch?"

She glanced at him. "It's not unheard of. He's a good guy. I send his family a Christmas card every year and get a picture of them. They're still in Ohio."

"But you came back to Crystal Cove even though your family and…you came back."

"It was home. I still have friends here."

"And you're still friends with your ex."

She chuckled at his obvious jealousy. It made him look vulnerable and endearing with that little dip of his head as he spoke.

"Yeah, from afar. Is that really such a strange thing?"

"I'm just wondering why we couldn't be friends all these years."

"You were different," she said quietly.

"I'm not kind?"

"I didn't say that. It's just…I never loved Rafe the way I loved you. There, I said it. Happy now? Anything else you're wondering?"

"Did you get that tattoo over your heart for him?"

She snapped her gaze at him, shocked. "We're back to the tattoo? I told you it was private."

"What type of tattoo? I mean, I know it's there. I saw part of it."

"Why is it important?"

"I'm just curious."

"It's a tattoo. If you go to the supermarket, you'll see a hundred people with all kinds of tattoos all over their bodies. I have one little tattoo."

"I'm only interested in the one you chose to put on your beautiful left breast."

She fought hard not to let the tears that were burning her eyes win. She couldn't let them. And she couldn't tell him about the delicate butterfly tattoo with the hidden symbol inside. Most people wouldn't notice it. The artist who'd created the work of art on her left breast made sure it wasn't easy to see. But Meredith knew it was there.

She couldn't talk about it or the fact that she'd cried for days afterward, so much so that she couldn't even look at the tattoo except to put ointment on it so it wouldn't get infected as it healed. She couldn't say the words, so she deflected.

"What about you? Did you ever get married? Have children?"

"I almost got married. It was many years after us. I'd just been promoted to Major. Karen was as keen on my career ambition as you were. She was in the military herself, so I'd always assumed she understood."

"She wanted you to change?"

"Her goal was to stop dating," he chuckled wryly and shook his head. "I didn't share that goal, at least not with her."

As he spoke, Meredith let herself look at him for the first time without turning away every time a memory came to her mind. His short-cropped hair was still thick on his head but was so different from the long hair he'd had when they'd dated before he'd gone to boot camp. The wind whipped strands of her hair around her face, but not a hair on his head moved. Everything about him seemed so controlled.

"I was fine the way we were," he continued, seemingly unaware of her staring. "We were together off and on for over a decade. It was comfortable. Easy to be together. Easy to be apart. I should have known better. My marriage has always been the military."

Try as she may, Meredith couldn't squash the sadness that washed over her. She'd never felt this raw after breaking up with Rafe. Everything was so amicable. There'd been a few tears, sure. But she'd cried endlessly when Griffin told her he'd signed on for four more years in the Air Force. And then even more when she'd sent off that letter ending things.

Drawing in a deep breath of ocean air, she fought to

smooth over the raw edges she convinced herself had healed years ago. Oh, boy, could Meredith lie to herself. One morning dancing in a park with Griffin, and she was a puddle. She wasn't crying. She hated doing that in front of people. But she would later. Right now, every inch of her felt exposed.

After a long ride of eating and filling in a few blanks for each other about jobs and places they'd been, they reached Crystal Cove. The hotel was only a few miles away. The sun was still high enough in the sky at midday to be hot. In the open SUV, she should have had a hat on. The tender spots on her cheeks told her she already had a sunburn, so putting one on now would do her no good.

Griffin pulled up to the front of the hotel turnaround and shoved the stick shift into park.

"Thank you for coming with me today."

"Honestly, I'm glad you pushed me. It was good, right? We were good?'

He smiled. "Yes. Although my curiosity about that tattoo is still killing me."

"Then you'll be dead by midnight because I'm not telling you."

He laughed as he stepped out of the Jeep. She didn't wait for him to open her door. She got out on her own.

"So about tonight." He reached for her, leaning in a way that was so familiar. But she'd be lost in him if she didn't stop it now.

She placed a finger against his lips. He *had* been ready to kiss her. But this time, she had to stop him.

"Today was pretty great," she said.

"I'm glad you think so."

"Let's not ruin it by making it linger too long." The

disappointment in his eyes was unmistakable. "Can we just sit with this a while?"

Griffin kissed her finger, and she pulled it away.

"You're going to make me sing karaoke all by myself tonight? You don't want to be there to laugh at me?"

She smiled. "I'd love to be a fly on the wall. But I need some time. Besides, I hear Betsy Womack was on the planning committee. She's still a real stickler for rules."

"What rules? You'll be my date."

She groaned.

"Come with me."

She raised an eyebrow and chuckled. "Is that a command? You look all official, Colonel."

"Not at all. A request. I'm not even in uniform."

"People talk, Griffin. They'll assume things."

"Since when do you care about what people say?"

"Okay, how about this? You'll leave here after this weekend, and I'll still be here. I was here when you left for the military and was here after we broke up, at least for a while. It wasn't pleasant. People say they're being supportive, but it's still just gossip. I didn't like it then. I'm not sure I'd be any good at it now."

They reached the back door of the resort that led to the lobby. They'd already passed the walkway to the elevator that would take Griffin to his room.

"So that's a no? Tell me you aren't even the least bit curious about people we went to school with."

"Maybe a few who'd moved away like we did. But..."

"But?"

She sighed. "Goodbye, Griffin. It really was good seeing you."

"No, no goodbyes. In Hawaii, we say aloha. So, I'm

going to say aloha, and when I see you again, I'll say aloha."

"What does that mean? The reunion is this weekend. You're going to be leaving in a few days."

"But not tomorrow. Tomorrow is another day."

"I'm going home. I have nothing to do at the hotel until Sunday, and even then, I've cleared everything with my staff. They can handle it. You won't run into me again here."

"Then I'll seek you out. I'm a determined man, Meredith. When I want something, I go after it. And I get it."

The melancholy that washed over her was filled with regret. If only he'd come after her thirty years ago. He would have had her.

CHAPTER 5

The one thing Meredith missed when she moved to Ohio was the beach. Not just any beach. She craved the white sands of the Florida's Atlantic Coast. In truth, she hadn't been to any other ocean beach. Most of the vacations she had were inland. She'd gone to Paris alone after her divorce from Rafe was finalized. She'd walked around thinking she had a big neon sign hovering over her head that said DIVORCED. She'd been on a skiing trip to Vale with a group of friends from her first corporate job. She still kept in touch with them and met them for dinner from time to time. But they had families and commitments she didn't have so it was hard to plan for those getaways and weekly dinners.

She suddenly realized she'd been spending way too much time alone. Today with Griffin had been the most fun she'd had in a long time, and they were visiting a memorial to a dead classmate! How had her life come to this?

The beach was her friend these days. Many days

after work, she'd walk home by way of the beach and leave her car at the hotel. She lived close enough to work to walk. She always kept clothes in her office at the hotel so she wouldn't be sweaty and gross after a long walk. After the day they'd had, leaving Griffin was the right thing, but it still left her empty.

So, she walked to the beach. She loved the feel of digging her bare feet deep in the warm sand until they sank into the cooler sand below as she walked. She loved the feel of her feet after the sand smoothed any rough spots on her skin, making it so soft. To any passersby, her walk along the beach probably looked ridiculous and would have been shamed by Mrs. Hughes, her dance teacher in her middle years. Of course, it hadn't taken much for Mrs. Hughes to shame her. She wasn't that great a dancer even after five years of trying. And she did.

But Meredith's lack of grace hadn't stopped her from dancing any more than it stopped her from walking in the sand in that awkward way of digging her toes in the sand and enjoying every step. With a gust of wind, the tendrils of hair that had become loose from her ponytail whipped around her face. She paused only to lift her face to the sun with her eyes closed to drink in the warmth. It was hot, not warm, this time of the year. But she'd long since reacclimated herself to the warmer weather since moving back to Crystal Cove after her divorce.

As she breathed in the ocean air, the stench of garbage floated around her, causing her to turn in the direction of the wind to find its source. Bingo. An overflowing garbage pail near the parking lot looked to be the source. She was glad it hadn't come from there as she approached the Ocean Vista. But the garbage can would be off-putting to guests who came to the beach.

Shoving her hand in her pocket, Meredith pulled out her cell phone. She tapped the number for the front desk of the Ocean Vista in her favorite contact list.

When the call connected, she said, "It's Meredith, Darcy."

"Hi. I thought you already left for the day."

"I did. I'm not working. I just went for a walk on the beach, but I'll be back to get my car."

"Can I do anything for you?"

Darcy was sweet, young, and eager to make something of herself. She wasn't going to last long at the Ocean Vista. She'd get a year or two of experience, enough to put on her resume and make it look good, and one of the other hotels down the coast would snatch her up with a higher-paying position. She'd go far if she kept at it.

"Please get one of the maintenance crews to come down to the beach parking lot to empty a few of the trash cans along the beach. Tell them it needs to be done right away."

"Isn't the town responsible for emptying those trash cans?"

"Yes, but it looks like no one emptied them last night, and now they stink to high heaven. It'll only get worse as it gets hotter. No one will want to be on the beach with this stink. The smell is going to head right toward the hotel."

"Right on it. I think David is still here."

"Great. Thank you."

"Oh, and Meredith?"

"Yes?"

"That hunky Colonel came down to the front desk looking for you."

"Griffin Cole?"

"Yes."

"What'd you tell him?"

"That I thought you'd gone home."

"Oh. Did he say what he wanted?"

"No."

"Okay." She sighed. "Make sure David gets right on it."

Meredith hung up the phone and hated herself for feeling so giddy that Griffin was looking for her. Damn. They'd spent the whole morning and early afternoon together, and he was still looking for her.

She actually wanted him to look for her and hated herself for it.

"You stupid girl."

Woman. She hadn't been a girl in a long time. She'd changed so much. So had Griffin. Despite the ease of them being together today, she could see it.

And yet the rapid beating of her heart and the smile she couldn't wipe off her face even if she deliberately put her hand to her mouth belied her. She was fifty years old, for God's sake! She had a failed marriage in her past. But it started long before that. Soon after things ended with Griffin, she'd made a decision that had haunted her for years and would probably haunt her to her grave. Despite throwing herself into college, graduating with honors and then achieving success in a big company she originally thought she'd work at throughout her life and retire in, life threw her curves.

She'd married and moved to Ohio. She'd found success in her career even though her marriage failed. She'd waited too long to come back to Crystal Cove. But when she finally made the move, she didn't want all that success anymore. It didn't matter. Three years after changing her career, she still couldn't quite remember the push for her to change and become an event planner, a job that paid a fraction of what she'd earned for years. But she knew it had something to do with happy people. She hadn't been happy for a long time. It was nice to be around people who looked forward to life. Who wanted to have fun, live, and plan for their future.

It made it possible for Meredith to live, too, if only through their excitement and happiness. It had been a considerable pay cut, but she'd done well over the years with investments and then with the inheritance she got after her parents passed away. She didn't need to work at all at this point. But the thought of not having something to go to every day while having nothing to come home to was too much to handle.

No, she didn't need the money. There was only so much money a person needed in life. She couldn't take it with her. At fifty-one years old, she had more than she needed, even if she decided to give up her Ocean Vista job and open a little micro-bakery.

She laughed as the thought popped into her mind. She rarely baked anymore. If she baked as much as she did when she was married, when the idea of a micro-bakery first came to her, she'd be double her size.

She stopped at a boulder on the edge of the parking lot and sat down. The rock was hotter than she'd expected and a little more jagged than her leg was happy about. She had to be careful not to tear her jeans. She had a clear view of the Ocean Vista's entrance. If Griffin emerged from there, he'd see her. But the likelihood of him being there was small. The events of the class reunion had started. She'd read the chatter on social media earlier from people from Griffin's class who had already arrived in town for the reunion. A few of her high school friends from the Class of 1989 had reached out to her to see if she would be around. Some she hadn't seen since high school. Some of them were people who'd been invited to Griffin and Meredith's wedding, but that never happened.

The garbage can was truly becoming offensive. But now it was mixing in with the smell of the steak house at the corner of the strip, which was now in full swing for the dinner crowd. She turned to the sound of shoes pounding on the pavement, getting louder as the person running came closer. She turned to find a tall and lanky young man running up to her with two large black garbage bags.

She sighed.

"David, what are you going to do with those?" Meredith asked.

"Darcy said you needed me to pick up trash."

David didn't even have the decency to be out of breath after that run. She chuckled and shook her head. He was young but eager to work and would do well. And God help her, she had a sweet spot for him because he was such a nice young man.

"I had expected you to get one of the garbage bins on wheels, but I guess that will do."

He looked around. "Doesn't the town take care of the beach?"

She lifted an eyebrow. She wasn't his boss, but she did feel a sense of authority over the younger workers and felt responsible for them because she knew someone else—Edward—wouldn't teach them. He'd just yell at them. She'd seen it happen before. More than a few good workers quit after a lack of nurturing made them feel like failures.

"I'll get right on it," David said, his shoulders slightly sagging and his curly brown hair whipping around his head with the sudden gust of wind that pushed the stench of the garbage away from her nostrils.

"Thank you. It's a bad look for the hotel if the beach stinks. I'll have Edward call the town hall, so you won't have to do it again."

He waved at her as he ran toward the first garbage pail. David wasn't like some of the young ones who'd worked at the Ocean Vista for the summer. Some stayed a few months and then left. It wasn't sexy enough or fun for them. They weren't ready to do real work. But David was a good worker, and she didn't want to see him leave for the wrong reason. He'd been raised by a single mom who worked a lot, and it was clear from his dedication that her example had rubbed off on him. Meredith would make sure Edward knew of David's extra effort.

Her shirt was soaked from the sweat of walking and sitting in the hot sun. She ran her tongue over her lips to help relieve the dryness, but her mouth was cotton-dry.

Holding a full trash bag he'd just filled, David paused about thirty feet from her as he returned to the hotel. "I can get you a bottle of water, Ms. Prichard. You don't look so good."

"Is that right?"

She forced herself not to be offended, especially since she wasn't sure exactly what he meant by not looking so good. But it was sweet that he offered.

"Thank you, David. I think I'll just go there myself and get something from the hotel store. Great job today. I'm sure Edward will appreciate it."

Being careful not to rip her jeans, Meredith eased off the rock and brushed her behind with his hand to remove any sand. She took one step toward the hotel and felt what David meant by her not looking good. She definitely needed to hydrate.

As she walked through the revolving doors, her face was immediately bathed with the cooler air, relieving the lightheadedness she'd felt on the walk back to the hotel. She had some sodas in the mini fridge in her office. But she decided to go to the hotel's little store to grab a bottle of juice. She was just finishing the bottle when Griffin appeared in the lobby.

"You're here!" he said. "I thought I was going to have to bribe Raymond to give me your address."

"It would have cost you. Raymond isn't easy to win over about such things."

He smiled. "You know, this would be a whole lot easier for me if you just gave me your cell number."

"I wasn't aware that I was supposed to make things easy for you."

"You still like to play hard to get."

"As I recall, it wasn't all that hard. I practically fell at your feet during my freshman year's first football game."

"Ah, that's right. You did that. I thought you were just clumsy."

Shaking her head, she said, "Is that right?"

"Don't worry. I didn't think that for very long. I'm still hoping to convince you to come to the Karaoke night. I really don't want to go alone. Or we can skip it all together and just spend the night—"

"It's not a good idea," she said, cutting him off. "I thought we agreed."

"We did. But I don't care if people talk. They're going to talk one way or another. You know that."

She did.

"Come on. We might as well have some fun with it. I say we give the entire Class of 1989 something to chew hay on. Create a scandal. Then sit back and watch them tell stories."

She chuckled. "You're so mean. They're your friends."

"Yours, too. You knew a lot of them. You have to admit it could be fun."

"If not humiliating."

"Well, that's the fun. Say you'll come with me? Please?"

She drew in a deep breath and couldn't wipe the smile she knew was on her face. "When you say it like that, how can I resist?"

"Great!"

"There's just one problem."

"What's that?"

"Look at me. I'm gross. I'm sweaty from walking on the beach and being out in the sun. And I can't exactly go to an event like this when you…" She gestured to his clothes. Unlike this afternoon, Griffin was dressed in what she guessed would be considered business casual: a button-down long-sleeved shirt with tie and no jacket. His pants were much more formal than the blue jeans he'd worn earlier but fit snugly against his hips and behind. She liked the laid-back version of him better. But he'd look amazing wearing anything.

"I'll wait. We can go back to your place so you can shower and change and then go to the Hawthorne House from there."

"Meredith?"

At the sound of Edward's voice, Meredith grabbed Griffin's hand. "No time. We have to run."

"What?"

"That's my boss calling me. I'm not supposed to be here. If I don't leave here now and he finds me, I'll never get out of here tonight. Run with me."

As she headed to the revolving doors, she tugged on

his arm until they were both snug inside the same capsule as the door moved. He pulled her close against him, and then, in a woosh, they were outside, and he let go.

It was so sudden, and her body reacted so strongly to the close proximity that it left her dazed.

Griffin looked at her quizzically and said, "I didn't want you to get caught in the door."

"Oh. My office is over in the next building."

"Your office? I can drive you to your place to get dressed."

She took him by the hand and tugged him until he followed her behind a cluster of bushes against the building. "I keep a change of clothes in my office. I can shower in the pool area. All I need is fifteen minutes. I can get myself together and then meet you in the parking lot by the Jeep, so Edward won't find me."

"Edward?"

"My boss. Trust me. It's quicker this way."

Meredith slipped into her office and shut the door quietly, hoping and praying Edward wouldn't wander around looking for her since she hadn't acknowledged him earlier. Her desk phone rang, and she cringed. Glancing at the caller ID, she saw that it was Darcy.

"What do you need, Darcy?" she whispered into the phone after answering it.

"Is something wrong?"

"You called me."

"Edward has been screaming about where you are. He heard your voice and knew you were still here. You're not answering your cell phone."

"With reason."

"Edward is headed to your office. Should I tell him—"

"No! No, do not tell him I am here. I am just getting a few things straightened out on my desk, and then I'm leaving. I have plans tonight."

"With the hottie Colonel?" she whispered.

She couldn't argue with that. "Yes, the hottie Colonel. Don't tell Edward you talked with me. Don't tell him you saw me. If you see Colonel Cole walking around in the next ten minutes, tell him to meet me outside by the hammocks instead of by the Jeep. With my luck, Edward will be waiting in the parking lot for me. Darcy, say it quietly so no one hears. Can you do that?"

"Sure thing."

"Make sure you don't tell Edward."

"Do you want me to distract him, so he doesn't find you in your office?"

"I'd love you if you can do that."

She giggled. "I'll take care of it."

Thank you, Darcy!

Opening the coat closet, she pushed a few outfits aside and inspected them. Keeping a cocktail dress or two in her office in case there was an emergency and she was needed out in public during a hotel event was a must and had saved her a time or two. It was more professional than wearing blue jeans or office attire if she needed to mill around the guests during an event. After several seconds of inspection, she decided on a black dress that might work with a pair of shoes she had previously chosen for another outfit. They'd still work. The pumps were three inches high. She hadn't worn pumps this high at work in years. It would do for a night out, though.

Draping the dress over her arm and hooking the sling-back shoes on her fingers, she bent down and rummaged through her drawer for something she could use to hold her wallet. She'd left the house with just her wallet shoved in her pocket. Her keys were clipped to the wallet. Biting her lip, she thought for a second. She didn't have time to stop at the hotel store and get something appropriate to use as a handbag. She doubted they even had something that would fit the bill, and she still ran the risk of Edward finding her.

She'd make do with her wallet and keys no matter how ridiculous it looked with the dress. She doubted anyone would pay any mind.

After cracking her office door, she eased into the hallway to ensure she didn't hear Edward walking around. She could hear his voice booming as he spoke to someone in the banquet room.

Meredith took a chance and raced across the courtyard barefoot, holding her clothes in her hand. It was her chance to get across the courtyard to the pool room so she could shower and get dressed without Edward seeing her wandering the halls. As she passed by the front desk, she leaned over the counter and spoke softly to Darcy. "I'm going to be five minutes. Ten minutes tops in the shower room. Can you pick up my clothes from there? I don't want to come back around this way."

"Sure thing, Meredith."

"Great. Leave everything in my office, and I'll deal with it later."

"Okay. Have a good time with the hottie Colonel." Darcy giggled.

"I owe you."

Twenty minutes later, Meredith walked toward the hammocks where she'd first seen Griffin just days before. Her heartbeat hammered in her ear as her blood flowed through her veins. Only this man had ever been able to make her feel as if she were having a full-blown heart attack just standing near him. Moving too quickly in the three-inch pumps, her foot hit a dip in the walkway, and her ankle began to twist sideways, but she managed to right herself just as Griffin turned around and saw her coming his way. His lips curled into a smile that made her catch her breath.

"Are you okay?" he asked, coming toward her.

"You saw that, huh?"

"The tail end of it."

"I'm fine. I must do that at least once a day on this walkway. It's nothing."

And it was a lie.

Griffin didn't say the words, but she could see it in his expression and the slight intake of breath as his gaze swept over her. She was beautiful despite nearly falling on her face.

"Do you have any idea how much I want to kiss you right now?"

She was playing with fire, and she knew by the end of his weekend, she'd get burned. Bad. But Meredith didn't care.

Reaching up and wrapping her arms around his broad shoulders, she said, "I've been regretting stopping you this afternoon ever since you left me. I figured if you didn't try again, I'd have to make the next move myself."

His lips curled into a grin. His voice was low and smooth, like a caress over her skin. "I like the sound of that."

Her breath hitched as his head came down to meet hers. He gently cupped her cheek with the tips of his fingers and brushed his lips over hers. At first, it was gentle. He was waiting for her to respond. She knew him so well even now. And then she could feel him grow hungry for more and it matched the building passion she felt deep in her soul.

Reaching up, she placed her hand behind his neck and pulled him closer to her even though their lips were locked in a kiss. As a soft groan made its way up her throat, he pressed his tongue against her lips to open her mouth, and then he claimed her with his tongue, moving it intimately with hers and building her excitement until she wanted him more. Needed him. And she remembered what it was like to be in his arms and be lost in him and him in her. God help her, she wanted to make love with him. It was hard to stop at a single kiss when she knew what the whole deal felt like.

When they parted and he looked down into her eyes, she felt as if he were looking into her soul, seeing the secrets she'd fought so hard not to reveal and claiming her as his. It was as if the last thirty years had never happened.

CHAPTER 6

They drove to the Hawthorne House. Despite being the second day of the class reunion, this was the first time she'd seen many of the people she'd grown up with and hadn't seen since high school.

Karaoke. How did she let Griffin talk her into this? Well, she didn't have to get up on stage and sing. She could reconnect with some old friends and mill about with Griffin. There would be talk. There always was, and the years wouldn't make it any different. Besides, word had already gotten out that Griffin was in town, and they'd been seen together, thanks to social media posts about the class reunion.

But Meredith refused to be the source of gossip. Despite being in a different building, she was surrounded by familiar faces that brought back shared memories.

"Hey, Colonel! It's Colonel, right?"

"Good to see you, Jared."

"You ended up making the Air Force a career. How did that work out for you?"

Jared Slocum had always been status-conscious. Age

hadn't changed him. He'd never been subtle in asking about someone's personal business.

"Living the dream in Hawaii."

Jared's eyes widen. "Paradise, huh? That has to hurt financially. What about you, Meredith? Last I heard, you were working in some big marketing job. What company are you with now?"

"I didn't realize you were keeping tabs on me, Jared."

He laughed as he touched his slightly bald head while trying to keep his drink upright with the other hand. At one point, the top of his head was a riot of curls. Now, it had thinned to just wisps. "I keep tabs on everyone. You got to know who your competition is."

"Everyone is the competition?" Griffin said. "Even old friends?"

"What's a little competition between friends? Looks like Meredith did you double."

"Excuse me?" they said in unison.

"CEO of marketing. Am I right? Wow! That's bank. What were you? Mid-six figures with bennies?"

"Why does it matter?"

"It doesn't. Just curious." He turned to Griffin. "That has to pay more than double or triple that of a Colonel, right?"

"I wouldn't know," Griffin said.

"It's a good thing old friends don't care about such things," Meredith added. "It's good seeing you, Jared."

Meredith pulled Griffin's arm to move on to another group of people. Jared's protests grew more faint as they walked on. "Oh, come on. I was only kidding. It's good seeing you two love birds together."

Reading the expression on Griffin's face was hard. She knew him too well.

"Don't listen to him," she said. "Jared has always

been on a status trip. I thought age would have made him less of a jerk. It looks like nothing's changed."

"He's right, though."

She stopped walking short of meeting up with a group she recognized. "How?"

"You were the CEO of marketing? That *is* impressive. Really big. Now, you work as an event planner."

"I like working as an event planner. Is there anything wrong with doing a job you like?"

"No. But CEO of marketing! Jared wasn't wrong. It does make quite a bit more than an Air Force Colonel. And quite a lot more than an event planner."

She scrutinized his face. "Does that bother you?"

"No. Not at all. But I can't help but wonder why you left such an important job."

"To do what? A job that is not important?"

He shook his head. "No, that's not what I mean. I am sure the people you work with are grateful for your expertise. You said you enjoyed it. That's all that matters. I certainly wouldn't know the first thing about throwing a party for more than five people unless it's a BBQ. And even then, I need the local butcher to help me with how much meat to buy."

Her lips were resistant, but they finally stretched into a smile. "It's a job, Griffin. I had a well-paying job for a long time. I was good at it. But after a while, I wanted to cry every morning when I woke up. Being good at something doesn't mean you enjoy doing it. Now, I have a job that doesn't make nearly as much money, but it makes me smile when I see happy people. I don't miss my old job even a little. It served me well. I never even think about it anymore."

"Was it a problem when you were married?"

"What?"

"The amount of money you made."

His words felt like a gut punch. "Not for me."

"But for your husband."

"Ex-husband. And maybe." They'd already talked about Rafe. But suddenly, Meredith felt so exposed talking about him in a room full of people, even though none of them were paying attention to her except for Griffin. "I don't know. Rafe never really talked about it. He did very well on his own."

Rafe had never wanted to talk about money. He'd been very old-fashioned. He wanted to be able to provide for her, and he did. He never asked about her salary. He never asked how she invested her money, either. He'd insisted she keep her money separate. She'd made good investments, and Rafe was shocked when she divulged her assets in the paperwork during their divorce. He'd rejected her proposal to split their assets equally. He hadn't wanted any of the money she'd invested.

"Money has broken up a lot of marriages," Griffin said.

"We're not married."

"No. But that is only because you broke things off."

"Why are we talking about this? Would it have been a problem if we were married?"

"I told you it wasn't a problem."

"Then why are you letting someone like Jared rattle you about money."

His smile was slow. But then he sighed and said, "I'm being ridiculous. I don't know how to say this without sounding sexist or condescending."

"Then just say it, and I'll decide how to feel."

"You never needed me. I can see that now. But somehow, all these years, I just assumed…"

"That I needed you?"

"Yeah."

"I did need you for a long time."

"Then you didn't."

"I figured out a way not to need you. It wasn't easy."

He drew in a deep breath. "We came here to sing, didn't we?"

"No, you came here to sing. I'm just here for the free food and the laughs."

Griffin's phone rang. It was hard to hear it above the noise in the room, and nearly impossible to hear the ring when the music started. But as he pulled the phone out of his pocket, the bright screen lighting up made it unmistakable. He quickly pressed a button and put the phone back in his pocket.

It took a drink or two, but after a few of the classmates got up and sang, somehow Griffin and Meredith got the courage to get up on the stage for a rendition of *Money for Nothing* by Dire Straights. They laughed through most of it and danced as they did at Dames Point Park, as if no one was watching. But they reached the end and came off the stage laughing like fools walking hand in hand. When the music died down again, the ringtone of Griffin's phone pealing rose above the sound of the laughter in the crowd.

Griffin glanced at the caller ID, hit a button and then shoved his phone in his pocket.

"That's the second time you've done that," she said.

"It can wait."

"Are you sure? Sounds like someone clearly wants your attention."

"It's…I'll call back."

Meredith hadn't been prone to jealousy for many years, but somehow, it crept through her veins and coiled around her, squeezing at her chest. She loathed the feeling.

What did Griffin say was the name of his ex? Karen? Or maybe there was someone new in his life. Damn her for wondering.

The phone rang again, and Meredith said, "Oh, for God's sake, just take the call. You know, it could be a world crisis or something," she said, trying to stay light.

"It's not. It's…personal."

After all that laughter, her mood soured. "It's okay. I'm going to get a drink. Maybe get drunk now that I've completed my contribution to this week's social media circus by making a fool of myself at your class reunion. You can call back whoever has been hounding you all night. I'll get a beer for you?"

"Sure."

Griffin watched Meredith's hips sway as she walked toward the bar and let his gaze linger, enjoying the view. Normally, he would get the drinks instead of letting her navigate the crowded bar. But Lucas was anxious. Griffin knew he would be. He'd already called four times tonight.

He couldn't put off talking to Lucas any longer.

Walking to the doorway, Griffin watched Meredith talk with Gabby Collins at the bar and hit Lucas's number on his favorites list.

"Hey," he said, answering the phone.

"How's it going?" Lucas asked.

"Karaoke tonight. Picture your most humiliating nightmare. I'll be sure to send you videos. Someone must be posting a bunch on social media as we speak."

"I can't wait." Lucas laughed, which brought a smile to Griffin's face and washed away some of the anxiety he'd been feeling about what was coming next.

"Have you said anything yet?"

His stomach fell. "Not yet."

Silence.

"I will, Lucas. Not tonight, but…maybe tomorrow."

"You only have a few days left."

"I will."

"What's she like?"

"I've already told you. Many times."

"No, you told me about a twenty-year-old girl you almost married. I want to know what she's like now."

He saw Meredith searching the room for him. "I'll get back to you on that. Just give me some time."

A few minutes later, Meredith handed Griffin his beer. "Rumor has it there will be a rendition of *We Are the World*. Do you want in on it?"

"Definitely. But not if they wait until the end of the night when everyone is too drunk to sing."

"I draw the line if Gabby pushes one of us to sing any Journey song. She's on a mission to get someone to sing *Open Arms* so she can recreate her prom dance with Jared."

"Interesting."

"Not." She took a sip of her drink. "Phone call taken care of? Is the world order unraveling?"

She had questions in her eyes. He had to tell her about Lucas. He was just being a coward, and there was no reason he should be. He hadn't done anything wrong.

"No world crisis."

"Good to know."

Just as the tension seemed insurmountable, music began to blare over the speakers, and a group of classmates ran onto the dance floor.

"Who's singing?" Gabby yelled into the microphone.

"Has Sean shown up yet? He did such a great concert on the beach earlier, and I'm hoping to get more of that tonight."

Sean West was one of the classmates who always dreamed of making it big in the music industry. And he did exactly that using the stage name Sammy Fedder with his band.

Meredith leaned into him. "I missed the concert on the beach. It must have wrapped up by the time I took my walk. I'm sure he sang his top song, *Born to Be My Baby*."

"I forgot about that one," Griffin said, leaning into her.

"When it was released, it played endlessly in every store and restaurant in Crystal Cove. People were so excited that a local boy had made it big in music."

"Come on, everyone," Gabby called out from on the stage. "Let's get Sean on the phone and convince him to come up to the stage. I know some of you have his cell number."

The music started playing again, and the crowd started dancing.

"*Love Shack*?" Meredith said, glancing at Griffin.

"Not exactly Sean's or Sammy Fender's style."

"He's always going to be Sean to me."

"How about I snatch a bottle of wine from the bar, and we get out of here before Gabby starts looking desperate?"

"Sounds like a plan. Gabby's determined to get Sean here to sing one of his songs tonight. It might get ugly."

"I did see Violet Slyk earlier. At least, I think it was her."

"It was," Meredith confirmed. "They were on the beach for the concert and filmed a segment for their show *Chart Toppers in Music*. The kids at the hotel were talking about it. The feature must have been Sammy Fender."

"Everyone seems like they're on their way to getting drunk. No one will care if we slip out and get drunk on the beach by ourselves."

"Let's get out of here."

Griffin walked over to the bar and talked with one of the bartenders. After exchanging money, he slipped a bottle into his jacket and returned to Meredith.

"Beach or the jetty?" he asked.

"Rocks and alcohol don't sound like a good plan."

"Point taken."

Within minutes, they slipped out the side door. He ignored the few inquiring glances they got when they saw Griffin and Meredith together. He heard his name being called, but he ignored it. He was sure he'd connect with whoever called him at the Glory Days banquet tomorrow night, so it was easier to pretend he hadn't heard.

Connecting with old friends he shared history with was fun. But the woman who'd pulled off her shoes and held them in each hand as she danced to the music barefoot as they left commanded all his attention. The beauty who dug her toes in the sand and swayed her body back and forth playfully. She'd been his best friend, and he'd forgotten just how much he'd missed that until he revisited old memories by creating a new one as if the years between them had never happened.

He didn't recognize himself much these last few days. He wasn't this man who was afraid of talking to a woman. Any woman. Or bringing up a difficult subject. He dealt with difficult circumstances all the time.

But that was him, and he loathed himself for it.

Meredith spun around to face him. "Hey, you didn't happen to swipe any glasses, did you?"

He shook his head as he pulled at his tie to loosen it. "I was more concerned with getting something that didn't need a corkscrew."

Meredith laughed as she twirled. "Good thinking. We don't want to make that mistake again."

She ran her fingers through her hair as the wind whipped her dress back as they walked toward the surf. The sun had long since sunk behind them, and there was nothing but blackness. What they could make out was lit by the lights behind them from the hotel leading to the water.

"Oh, I love the ocean. I hated living in Ohio because I could never get my feet in the sand. The beach is so therapeutic, don't you think?"

She turned to him and stumbled just a bit. She was giddy, happy, and on her way to tying on a good drunk. He was way behind her and wasn't sure this bottle would help him get there. But Griffin laughed as he watched Meredith.

He'd forgotten. He'd loved this wild and carefree part of Meredith. He…he'd loved *her*. How insanely crazy was that after all these years? No matter how he tried to pretend he had aged and moved on, he still did couldn't shake the feeling that it had always been there and my God, he still loved her as he did over thirty years ago. Maybe it was just memories unearthing themselves from a deep part of his brain. Maybe they belonged there, not on the beach where it felt real.

But Griffin loved it as much as he loved that first peek of the sun in the morning over the water after he'd spent the night on his boat so he could catch paradise in the quiet while drinking his first cup of coffee. There was still so much left unsaid between the two of them. There was so much he wanted to discover about who Meredith had become. He'd known the girl. But this woman was intoxicating. They'd lived more years apart than they'd shared, and he couldn't wait to discover what had formed her into this incredible beauty.

Memories of the last time they'd been on the beach at night swirled around his mind and clouded his judgment. Griffin should be telling Meredith about Lucas. But it would ruin the magic that was happening right now.

His time in Crystal Cove wasn't over. There was still time—tomorrow. Tonight, he just wanted to enjoy being with Meredith, a woman who had commanded his whole heart all these years, even if he didn't realize it.

"It's time for a swim," Griffin said.

"Are you crazy? I have a dress on." She laughed as she gazed at him for a long time. "Oh, no, no, no. You just want to see me naked."

"I can't see anything in the dark. But I can't deny that I wouldn't mind seeing you naked again."

"Nothing's changed except…"

"Except what?"

"I used to like my behind."

"It still looks good."

"Yeah? You checked it out?"

"I'm still me. You always had a great behind."

"It's covered in clothes. You haven't seen me naked in a long time."

"I thought I already confessed I wouldn't mind."

Her laughter floated into the air and swirled around him, making him dizzy. He could barely see her face, but he could feel her energy. It flowed through him. The slight change in her voice told a story he'd forgotten. He walked slowly toward her in the dark, listening to the music in the background. It was so far away, far enough that he didn't worry about being impulsive and taking Meredith in his arms the way he'd done years ago—the way he wanted to do it now.

"I think it's time for a little more wine, don't you think?" she said.

He'd forgotten about the wine he was gripping in his hand. It wasn't an expensive bottle of wine. They never stocked the bar with the good stuff during functions like a class reunion. But the screw top came off without a struggle, and when he pressed his lips to the mouth of the bottle, the first sip of wine went down his throat easily. Maybe too easy.

And then she was standing in front of him, and it was all he could do not to reach out to her and tangle his fingers in her wind-blown hair.

"You want to kiss me again," she said, taking the bottle from his hand.

"What makes you think that?"

"Because I know you, Griffin Cole. You like kissing me."

"I do?"

She took a long drink. "You absolutely do."

His chuckle rumbled in his chest as desire stirred inside him until he felt his whole body hum.

"What makes you so sure?"

She pointed a finger at him. "I know that look even though it's hard to see in the dark. And we're both going to taste good with wine on our tongues."

His body immediately responded to her words, and he felt himself grow hard. He could barely see it in the dark and wondered how she could possibly see any expression on his face. Even though he couldn't see her with his eyes, his mind wandered to the way her head tilted to one side when she was looking up at him and the way she pursed her lips as if she were about to lay a few humorous words directed at him before she kissed him. They were old memories, but they lived so close to the surface of his mind that it was hard to ignore, even in the dark.

What he wanted would complicate everything. It was reckless. And he didn't care. They had a lot to discuss, not the least of which was what was happening between them now. He wasn't exactly sure what that was.

He'd been a fool. Time had not erased the pain. Anger had not replaced the love. It had only served to mask what he didn't want to accept. One look at Meredith, and all those feelings of love came rushing back. He'd never been over her. He'd just disappeared in his career in the military, the very thing that had caused their split up all those years ago.

"You're so beautiful," he finally said. That wasn't what he wanted to say. What he wanted would only complicate things more than he dared.

"You can't see me," she said quietly.

"I see you all the time. I hear your voice all the time in my mind. I didn't realize how much until I came here. It's never left me, Meredith. You are in me."

She dragged her bare feet in the sand. He still had his shoes on, and the sand was spilling in, pressing against his feet and making his shoes uncomfortable. But he didn't care. He wanted to kiss her.

"I think that's the wine talking," she said so quietly he almost didn't hear it over the sound of the surf crashing into the beach. "But I like you saying it."

"Do you, now."

She chuckled and came close to him, running the flat of her palm across his chest. "I do."

Those words had haunted him. They'd never been able to say them in front of family and friends. Now the words rolled off her tongue as if...

Who knew what life would have brought them if she'd been honest with him, if Meredith hadn't angrily walked away without telling him why she was ending a romance that he'd depended on in so many ways while he'd been in Iraq?

"I'm going to let you kiss me, Colonel Griffin Cole," she said.

He reached for her and put his fingers on her arm as she moved. He didn't claim her. He had no right. It had been too long since he'd been comfortable dragging her into his arms and covering her lips with his with the kind of hunger he felt now.

"For the record, I think it's a bad idea," she said as she stepped forward.

"Then why are we doing it?"

She was so close, and he had to fight to keep himself from being too demanding. Meredith liked the dance. He'd forgotten how fun that was, if not maddening.

Reaching up, she placed her hands on his shoulders and lifted on her toes. He bent his head, and his mouth was only inches from her lips.

"Because I want to. I've missed kissing you."

Somehow, she was in his arms, and his fingers were tangled in her hair as the wind whipped it around their faces. He wasted no time crushing her lips with his and tasting her. She didn't just taste like the wine they'd been drinking. It was her, a sweet drug that filled him completely as he coaxed her lips apart with his tongue and joined hers.

He could swear he heard the soft moan rise in her throat above the sound of the pounding surf. His fingers itched to touch the spot where her pleasure rumbled and made him want to drop to the sand and take her. He kissed her deeply as she melded into him as if they were one. And when they parted, he wanted more. He wanted it all. He wanted her. He'd always wanted Meredith.

She gazed up at him and said, "We're screwed."

CHAPTER 7

"Crap."

Meredith's eyes continued to flutter open as she took in the objects in the room. It wasn't her bedroom. It was the hotel. It had the familiar bedspread that was supposed to be neutral and pleasing, but she'd always thought it was drab and ugly. She recognized the generic artwork that was meant to blend into the wall space without being interesting or notable enough to want to look at it. It wasn't quite motel art, but it wasn't Monet.

Griffin walked out of the bathroom with a towel wrapped around his waist. "I left my shaving kit on the desk," he said nonchalantly.

"Oh."

"How do you feel?"

"Fine."

"Really? I'm pretty sure someone cracked an axe over my head. It reminds me why I don't drink wine anymore."

She pulled the drab comforter up to her chin. "Well,

now that you mention it, aside from the occasional glass of wine at dinner, neither do I."

"I called down to the front desk and asked Darcy to send up something for headaches."

"You called Darcy?"

He stopped at the bathroom door for a second. The towel lifted with his movement, and she was sure it would fall to the floor. "Yeah, bad idea?"

"No, Darcy is great. I need to hide, though. Better yet, I'll get out of here while you shower. I don't need my coworkers talking."

"You don't want her to know you're here?"

"Definitely not."

"Too late. I think she likes me."

She closed her eyes. "Oh, crap."

He frowned. "You don't want her to like me?

"No, she…never mind."

"What are you afraid of? Nothing happened."

"Why don't I believe that when I'm in your bed with…" Meredith lifted the comforter to see what articles of clothing she had on. "A bra and panties on."

"You didn't want to wrinkle your dress if you had to walk through the hotel to change."

"You mean I was thinking?"

He cocked his head to one side. "It may have been my idea. You look good."

"Shut up."

He chuckled. "Don't leave while I'm showering. I sent for breakfast. The woman in the kitchen said you like strong coffee and an egg white omelet with spinach and tomato."

"You talked to Angela about what I like for breakfast?" she protested. "I hate you."

"You didn't hate my last night when you were kissing me. By the way, I loved kissing the butterfly tattoo."

He smiled wickedly and then walked into the bathroom, closing the door.

"Oh, crap," she whispered, dropping her head back onto the pillow.

Within minutes, she found her dress hanging in the closet. She'd actually had the presence of mind to hang up her dress? Maybe Griffin did. She didn't remember coming to the room, much less undressing and climbing into bed.

She walked away from the closet to the middle of the room. A quick glance in the mirror had her wincing at her reflection as she listened to the sound of the shower running. Someone had to be banging on her head above her eye with a hammer. She was sure of it. Every step she took made her sway. She didn't drink like a young adult anymore. A glass of wine at dinner was usually her limit. Last night, they'd had a lot of wine, and her eyes showed it.

As the memory of walking back to the hotel became less fuzzy, she realized it also included a walk through the bar in her sandy bare feet to get another bottle. Glancing over at the desk where Griffin had just retrieved his shaving kit, she found two empty glasses with residual color on the bottom and an empty bottle of chardonnay.

The bottle was empty.

They weren't drinking chardonnay on the beach.

That made two bottles of different wine they'd polished off last night if they hadn't also raided the hotel room bar. No wonder her head pounded like a jackhammer.

She struggled with the zipper on her dress, pushing

grains of sand out of the zipper to unstick it. She was just about to rip off the whole dress when Griffin walked out of the bathroom.

He winked at her when she saw her half in the dress. "Need help with that?"

She turned her back to him and let him struggle with the zipper for a few seconds before it finally zipped it up to the middle of her back. "Room service hasn't arrived yet?"

"Um, no. I can't wait for breakfast. I have to go."

"You need to get some food in you."

"Eggs…I just can't. I need to get out of these clothes. I can't imagine what my staff will think when I walk back to my office in last night's clothes."

"You can put one of my shirts on."

"Over my dress? Oh, right, like that isn't a big neon sign for the 'Walk of Shame.'"

"We didn't do anything shameful. But we can."

"You're having too much fun with this."

He chuckled. "I'm enjoying it. I'll give you that. It's been a long time since you woke up in bed beside me."

"Um, about that."

"I told you. Nothing happened. I'm serious."

He looked at her, and she swore he had released a soft sigh of disappointment.

"I was in my underwear."

"I enjoyed that very much."

She cocked her head to one side, and he shrugged.

"You know I liked watching you in your underwear."

"You haven't done that in a long time."

"There is nothing for you to be embarrassed about. Although if we had made love, I'd be pretty devastated if you were embarrassed."

His cell phone began to vibrate and bounce all over

the nightstand. Griffin walked over to the nightstand and grabbed it before it fell onto the floor. After glancing at the caller ID, he shoved the phone in his pocket.

It may have been her throbbing head or the fact that the morning after never felt as magical as it did during the midnight hour, but Meredith glared at the phone. "That phone gets a lot of action."

"It can wait."

"Really? It keeps ringing, and I know someone on the other end of the line wants your attention. Maybe they don't like that you're giving that attention to me? Am I right?"

"Yes. But not the way you may be thinking."

She blew out a quick breath, suddenly overwhelmed by the events of the last twenty-four hours.

"It's none of my business. A few kisses and no sex doesn't mean you owe me any explanations. Someone you want to tell me about? I mean, not that you're obligated to tell me anything. That ship sailed a long time ago."

"You're right. I don't owe you. But you owe me."

"What? What do I owe you?"

"Forget it."

"There's no walking that back. Was that call the reason we didn't make love last night, even though I was practically half-naked in your bed? And don't say you didn't want to make love because I won't believe you."

"Of course I did. But you were drunk. So was I."

"That never stopped us before. In fact, I remember pretty great drunken hammock sex more than a few times."

His smile was quick, and it was hard to ignore that Griffin's mind raced to their shared memories.

"We were different then," he said. I'd like to think

I've changed—a little, anyway—for the better, I hope. Being with you makes me think the last thirty-plus years never happened."

She smiled weakly. The phone rang again.

"Oh, come on. Answer the phone. I'll leave you to it."

"I don't want you to leave. Breakfast will be here soon. I want to talk."

"Yeah, sure. I owe you."

"Yes."

She stared at him for a moment.

"Answer your phone. Whoever is on the other end of that line clearly needs you."

He pulled the phone out of his pocket and sighed. "He actually needs you. Well, maybe not need. He's pretty independent now. He's also very determined, as you can see."

The words were out of Griffin's mouth and caused the confusion he'd anticipated but suddenly wasn't prepared for. He'd rehearsed this conversation with Meredith in his head many times in Hawaii in the months leading up to the class reunion, and he still didn't know how to do it.

He was Colonel Griffin Cole, a United States Air Force commander. He had thousands of airmen who worked under him. He was responsible for them and their safety. And this phone call was more important than all that and the one he feared most.

"It's Lucas," he finally said.

She shook her head and frowned. "Lucas?"

"Our son, Meredith. Lucas is the son you gave up for adoption and never told me about."

Her face drained of color and panic filled her expression. She took a wide step back, swayed, and leaned against the desk for support.

"No," she whispered.

Oh, he wished that all the emotion and anger he'd felt when he initially found out about Lucas were gone, but her quick denial brought them back with a vengeance.

"Lucas. How do you…?"

"It doesn't matter how."

"The hell it doesn't!"

"Wait. Are you angry? At me?"

"Shocked."

"You can imagine my surprise when I learned I was a father, and you never told me."

"You weren't there." She spun away and looked at a blank part of the wall.

"This isn't buying a new car or getting takeout for dinner. This was…is a person that we created. You didn't think I'd want to know?"

"All this time…this is why you stayed at the hotel. This is the reason you came here."

"Of course. Lucas wanted me to come. He's been hounding me ever since his mother died."

"His mo…oh, no."

"He lost both his parents. I didn't want to come. But Lucas wanted me to."

"So, all this time you've spent with me was never about me or us. It was about you being upset that I never told you I gave a child up for adoption to a good home with two parents who were going to be there for him. Is that right?"

He frowned as his anger surged. "Don't make this about me."

His cell phone rang.

"Why not? You came here to what? Confront me?"

"If confronting you was all I wanted to do, I would have done it seven years ago."

"Seven? You've known about Lucas for seven years?"

"And what? I didn't tell you? I guess now we're even."

The cell phone rang again.

She began to pace in a way that makes a person crazy as if they would spontaneously combust with every step. He knew the feeling well.

"We've just spent days together. We spent all of last night sleeping next to each other, not that I remember much of it, but I woke up here half-naked, and you said nothing."

"Neither did you. Thirty years, and you said nothing to me. You broke things off and never said a word about being pregnant in your letter."

"Don't you dare judge me!"

"I think I have a right to."

"You weren't here. I was. My father had just died. My mother moved to Arizona, and my brother moved to New York. I was here alone waiting for you. I stayed here waiting for you. You were gone for years, and I trusted you'd return to me. I barely saw you. We rarely talked on the phone. I lived for the few days you had leave. And then you reenlisted for another four years without telling me until it was done. You didn't discuss it with me or ask how I'd feel about it. You just made a decision about what you wanted without regard to me or us."

"I would never have re-enlisted if you'd told me about him. I would have been there for you."

"But you weren't. Everyone was gone. Most of my friends went off to college. You have no idea the hell I went through alone here."

"Meredith."

"Don't Meredith me. Leave me alone." She began looking around the room for her shoes. She found one and considered just walking barefoot through the halls to her office. But that would attract more attention than her walking in the state she was in.

"You can't leave now. We have to talk."

"You lied to me. Again. Again, you lied to me."

"Don't you dare put this on me," he said, grabbing her by the arm to stop her. She pulled her arm away.

"Let me go. We have nothing to say."

"You know that's not true. There is so much we still haven't said to each other."

"Yeah? Do you know when a good time would have been to say something to me? How about thirty years ago before you re-enlisted just months before our wedding? How about the day you came back? That would have been a nice time. I have to go."

"You owe me this!"

His words stopped her in her tracks. She slowly turned around and leveled him with a stare that matched all the pain and anger she'd felt thirty years ago when she walked out of that hospital without their baby in her arms.

"I what?"

"You heard me."

"You must be remembering history wrong, Griffin. You disappeared on me. You left me and then kept choosing to leave me. I spent over thirty years agonizing over my decision to put our son up for adoption. I have one memory of holding him in my arms that had to last me a lifetime, and you come here now accusing me of owing you. Where were you?"

"You should have told me. I deserved to know and be there."

"You signed up for another tour, another war. You left me and our son behind, expecting us to wait until you were ready to share our life, the life you promised to share with me and never did. You left me. And then you kept leaving me. I don't owe you, Griffin. I…did what I had to do. You chose to leave us, and I had to make a very painful decision because I couldn't give our child what he needed."

"I would have been there."

"But you weren't. You were already talking about changing the wedding date. Again. I read the writing on the wall. The military won the coin toss. I don't think I was ever a serious choice."

"How can you say that?"

"How can I not say that given the fact I spent four years living for letters and phone calls that sporadically came? I planned things on my own. I spent all my time alone. And when you came home on leave, I lived for those moments. But those moments, the moment we conceived a child, were too few to drown out the loneliness of knowing I was being strung along and left behind. I wanted a life *with* you. I could have handled being your wife while you were in the military. I wanted to be part of our life together. But you never asked me about what I wanted. You made decisions and didn't even talk to me about them. You just did it. You signed up for another four years of me waiting around for you. You didn't give me a choice. So don't you dare stand there and judge me. I made a choice without you, yes. But you'd been doing that all along. You never cared about what I wanted or needed."

Not able to find her other shoe, she grabbed the one

shoe she found and decided to leave his room barefoot. Talk be damned.

With her heart pounding and tears stinging her eyes, she walked as fast as she could through the hallway, dodging a cart where housekeeping was already busy cleaning rooms. As soon as she reached the stairway, she pushed through the door and ran down the stairs as fast as she could.

She couldn't breathe.

She couldn't think.

He had known their son for seven years.

On the other end of that call was the son she'd given up for adoption.

How would he ever forgive her?

CHAPTER 8

She ran to her office, changed into yesterday's clothes, and got out of the hotel as quickly as she could. The touristy part of the main drag near the hotel was something Meredith had actually missed when she'd married Rafe. It was easy to get lost among the tourists. As she walked down the strip and glanced in the windows of the stores, meant to get as many tourist dollars as they could, memories flooded her.

It had been a long time since she'd walked the strip for any reason other than to get where she was going. But when she was a young girl with her friends, and then later, a young woman with Griffin, she'd always walked this strip. It was a place to be. It was where everyone was.

Her heart hurt as she walked, and she didn't know how to stop it. The familiarity of the slow walk, knowing no one on the strip knew her or cared why she was there, comforted her. It allowed her to revisit memories without feeling alone, even though no one cared what she was going through.

She smiled at an elderly couple holding hands as they

approached her. They were probably twenty-five or thirty years older than she was. Maybe more. Seeing their happiness as the woman laughed, pointing to a dress in the window, made Meredith envious. They were happy. Her mind wandered to a place that was probably inappropriate. They didn't need sex to be happy, but she wondered if they still loved each other that way, even in their later years. They were happy, in love, and their hearts didn't hurt like Meredith's.

She wanted that. Meredith wanted old people's sex. She wanted to hold hands while walking on the beach. Romance. She wanted to share her life with someone who made her catch her breath when he walked into a room.

She wanted Griffin. She'd always wanted that life with Griffin.

Meredith had spent years of being alone and being okay with it. She thought she was okay until Griffin walked into her life again. She hadn't given him much of a fight to spend time together, even after how things had ended. Even after all these years.

The elderly couple passed her, and suddenly, she felt the heat of the sun bearing down on her, pulling her to the ground. Realization was a hard thing to face. She'd been comfortable with being alone. She'd made her life, but until that moment, she hadn't realized that she hadn't been happy. She'd let herself slide into a place where she could fit her life into a box and say she was okay.

But she wasn't okay. She hadn't been for a long time. And now Griffin invaded that little box she'd made for herself and upended her world. Griffin was the man she wanted to have old people sex with. She wanted to have laughter on the beach and romance.

She had always envisioned a life with him and had buried the dreams of a young woman the moment she handed their son over to a social worker for someone else to claim as theirs.

The distraught expression on the faces of the younger couple approaching her caused her to stop.

"Ma'am are you okay?" the girl asked, stopping in front of her.

"Wha…excuse me?"

"You look like you're crying," she whispered, touching her arm in comfort. "Are you hurt? Can I help you?"

Meredith glanced at the young man with her as he kept his distance. He stared at her face with concern.

"I'm fine." She looked away at the building beyond them and then back at the woman's face. "It's sweet of you to ask. I guess the sun is getting to me."

"I can get you something to drink. Maybe you should sit in the shade for a while," the young man said, gesturing to the ice cream shop they'd just passed.

"I'm fine. So sweet of you to be concerned." She swiped her eyes and pretended it was sweat, pretended that the tears that were clearly covering her face, tears she hadn't realized she was shedding, weren't real. "I just need to get out of the sun."

The worry that remained on their faces let her know she hadn't convinced them. She'd been crying in public and wasn't even aware of it.

Wiping her cheeks again, she turned and walked back toward the ice cream shop. As she opened the door, a blanket of cool air hit her. The young couple followed her. The ice cream shop was packed. Young families filled up all the tables and seats with kids or couples who were probably strolling the strip as she was.

"Let me get you something to drink," the young man said.

"There's no need. I'm just going to go to the bathroom and splash some water on my face."

"Are you sure?" the girl asked.

"Yes, thank you so much."

Meredith headed to the bathroom. She passed a young family and saw a little boy of about three who couldn't sit still in his seat. He jumped off the bench and then climbed back on to look over to the counter where people were lined up waiting to be served ice cream by the counter help.

Her heart squeezed. She'd had a son, but she'd missed every single moment in his life. Had he been like this little boy? Active? Did he have a beautiful smile that looked just like Griffin's?

She reached the bathroom, pushed through the door, and gulped back a sob, thinking back to the day she'd had those few short hours with her child after he was born. She'd memorized the tiny features of his face. The little cleft chin and wide eyes were definitely Griffin. The moment he'd been placed in her arms, it was all she could see. Now, she wondered how much their son looked like his father.

Meredith had let him go. She'd had her reasons. At the time, she thought it was all she could do, but she couldn't think clearly about any of them now as she stared at her disastrous reflection in the bathroom mirror and cried. No wonder the young couple was so concerned. She was a mess.

Fifteen minutes later, Meredith emerged from the bathroom after giving her reflection a stern talk that had been witnessed by a mother and her young daughter she was potty training. There was no way around this. When it had mattered, Griffin wasn't there. He was halfway across the world. But he was in Crystal Cove now. He'd come here to tell her about their son, not to see her. There were moments over the last few days where she'd foolishly allowed herself to believe she'd been the reason. But no, it had been Lucas. She'd never even told him about Lucas, and he'd known for seven whole years.

Earlier, she'd been angry with Griffin. She had no right to be. She'd taken something from him without him even knowing. It was easy to see it that way now. And now, all these years later, she wasn't proud of the reason. She'd wanted to hurt him as much as she hurt. It was childish and reckless, and she had been the one who caused the pain. She could easily give the young girl she was some grace because she was no longer that girl and had matured. She knew more about what life could throw at a person. She'd buried both of her parents. She'd married and divorced without their guidance or support. She'd made a life for herself.

She couldn't give the woman she was now that same grace for her behavior this morning, hangover or no hangover.

She'd been wrong.

She needed to make it right—or as right as she could. She wasn't even sure it was possible to do that. But she had to confront Griffin. She had to let him be angry with her, and she needed to give him her reasons even if she wasn't that young, scared girl anymore.

She decided to walk the path toward the beach and returned to the hotel to get her car. As she walked, Meredith began to smell the stench of garbage again. Knowing exactly the problem, she headed back to the hotel quickly to have it rectified.

"Darcy, can you page David? The garbage barrels on

the edge of the beach are full again. He's not answering his phone."

The young girl had red-rimmed eyes. "Can't."

"What do you mean you can't?"

"Edward fired him." The drawn expression on her face told her it was true.

"What? What on earth for?"

Darcy shrugged. "I can call Rocko. He clocked in about an hour ago."

"What happened?"

She whispered. "It was awful. David was so upset."

Renewed anger surged through her. "Okay, call Rocko. I'm going to get to the bottom of what happened to cause Edward to fire David."

She wouldn't have stomped off with as much force as she did if not for the fact that Edward once again canned one of the better workers in this hotel. For a man who claimed to have big ideas, the man was an imbecile. And maybe that was an insult to imbeciles. She'd spent two months with him causing her headaches.

She headed down the office corridor behind the front desk until she reached Edward's office. The door was closed, as usual. Edward had never been an open-door kind of boss in the few months he had been here, and that was unlikely to change. It didn't matter today because she was going in.

She knocked on the door but didn't wait for him to answer before opening it enough to stick her body in the doorway. "A word?"

He glanced up from what looked like a finance report. On paper. There were sticky notes all over it. "Not now. I'm busy."

"I can see that. So am I, which is why I'm wondering

why you let go of the worker with the most potential to go far in this company."

"What?"

"David Rivera."

He shook his head in disgust and went back to the paperwork, which, upon closer inspection, showed red marks and sticky notes throughout. "Get out of my office, Meredith. I don't have time for this. Just get someone else to help you with whatever emergency you have."

"No, that's your job."

Lifting his gaze slowly, his stare bore into her. She didn't care. "Excuse me?"

"For the past few months since you started working here, I've been helping you try to fit into your position, knowing full well that I could do it better than you. You know it, and I know it. You rely on me. You wanted me to stick around to make the Ocean Vista an overflow hotel for a class reunion? One guest from that class is registered here. No events. And I had to wonder why. It's so you could hole up in this office and work on a financial report that is way past due."

"I noticed you have been spending time with that one guest."

"It figures you would hone in on that, not the real problem. But yeah, that's right. On my time. The rest of the time I'm picking up your slack. Why did you let go of David Rivera? He works harder than anyone else on staff. He has unlimited potential to one day take your job when you ditch this hotel for wherever you think you can get a better position."

"That's enough."

"That's right. I'm sick of going above and beyond for you when you make my life harder."

"The so-called hard worker you are talking about wanted a few days off. I couldn't give it to him, so he quit."

"Excuse me?"

"I told him if he left, I would take it as him quitting. So, it's on him."

"That's not the way Darcy saw it. Since you obviously had this conversation in front of other staff, I doubt the rest will also see it that way. Did he say why he needed the time?"

"His mother is in the hospital having surgery. I told him to wait until his shift was over."

"Edward! He's an only child of a single mother. Of course, he wants to be with her. If he had come to me."

"He didn't. You aren't his boss, no matter how much you think you are. You don't run this hotel. I do. I need people I can count on. Not people who go running out the door at the first emotional meltdown."

"Did he say it was serious?"

"What?"

"David's mother."

"Cancer or something."

"And you said no." Her mouth dropped open in shock. "How can you be so heartless?"

"You don't get ahead by taking in strays and letting them walk all over you."

"The people who work here are hardly strays. It's his mother, Edward."

He shuffled through some papers and came to a set with a yellow sticky note with her name on it in red marker.

"I need you to go through these and find out why they aren't balancing. Here. Take them."

Dutiful as always, Meredith grabbed the papers and

gave them a quick glance. Her mind wasn't on the papers, numbers, or the red marks on the columns. Poor David. He was just a young boy. If she had kept her Lucas, it could have easily been him. She wasn't sick, thank God. But the beautiful woman who'd raised him had died. And now David could be facing the same loss.

A few of the words on the page grabbed her attention. "These aren't my departments."

Edward turned to the computer and started typing an email. "I know."

She dropped the paperwork on his desk.

"I'm not doing your job for you, Edward. I meant it when I said I could do the job better than you because I've been doing it for you since you got here. No more."

"Meredith! Are you refusing to obey a command?"

"Oh, my God. Did you actually just say 'obey' to me?"

"This is insubordination. I have a good mind to fire you right now."

"But you won't because then you won't have someone to help you fix the mess you've made."

"Then take the reports."

"I quit."

Turning on her heels, she drew in a deep breath and waltzed out of the office listening to Edward's plea at her back and then a curse she was sure could be heard all the way into the lobby. As she passed Darcy at the front desk, Darcy giggled and said, "That was awesome."

It didn't feel awesome. "What's going on with David's mother?" she asked quietly.

"They called her in for surgery again." Darcy's eyes filled with tears. "They thought they got all the cancer before but...are you going to call him?"

"I don't want to intrude, but I figure he could use a friendly face right now."

"I think she's at County." Darcy nodded. "That's where she was before."

She nodded, then leaned forward toward the counter. "By the way, I quit. If you ever need a reference, make sure you call me. I'll give you one of my cards when I leave. I wish you the best of luck."

"You really quit?" Darcy's eyes bugged open.

"You quit?"

CHAPTER 9

eredith turned automatically to the sound of Griffin's voice. She immediately hated the fact that she was so glad to see him, she wanted to launch into his arms and have him hold her as he had last night.

And despite how horrible things were between them earlier, she still wanted him to hold her.

He took a step forward and placed his hands on her shoulders. No matter how she tried to keep them back, the tears came. "What's happened? Why did you quit your job?"

"It doesn't matter. But…"

"What happened? It's me. Just talk to me."

"I don't have time to talk. I need to go to County Hospital."

His expression immediately changed to panic. "The hospital? Are you okay?"

She leaned into him, and he took her into his arms. "No. I mean, yes. But I have to see David. I need to make sure he is okay."

"I'll take you."

"I have my car here."

"You aren't in any condition to drive. You're too upset. The least I can do is drive you."

Within a half hour, they were walking up to David's mother's hospital room.

"Maybe I shouldn't go in there," Griffin said. "David and his mother don't know me."

But I do, she thought. *And I need you in case this is bad.*

"You didn't have to come with me at all. Thank you for offering to drive, but you didn't have to come."

"You're upset. I don't want to leave you."

If that had always been true, things in their lives would look a lot different.

"I shouldn't have sprung things on you like that," he said regretfully. "In my head, it was supposed to go differently."

"That conversation is for another time," she said, looking at the hospital room number and recognizing David's voice as he joked with his mother.

"It's up to you. I'll only be a little while. I just want to make sure he is okay."

Griffin brushed his fingers against her cheek. "I'll wait out here."

She nodded and then knocked on the door. As she slowly walked into the room, she caught David sitting in a chair behind the drape in the second bed. His eyes lit up quickly and then shut down. He went from being the strong boy for his mother, laughing and joking, to the scared little boy afraid to lose her. Meredith's heart squeezed so tightly she couldn't breathe.

"Darcy said I could find you here," she said. "I hope I'm not intruding."

She glanced at David's mother in the bed. The

woman didn't look sick, but that meant nothing. Her hair was starting to see the effects of chemo. Soon people would be talking about shaving her head and wigs or rocking it bald. Something told Meredith immediately it would be the latter.

The woman smiled. "Are you a friend of David's?"

"I work with him. It's nice to meet you, Ms. Rivera."

She nodded. "He was just telling me stories about the Ocean Vista."

"Well, we really like David. He is a wonderful and delightful worker."

David looked down as if embarrassed.

"I just wanted to make sure you both were okay and to see if there is anything I can do to help you."

Ms. Rivera smiled weakly. "He just told me he doesn't have a job anymore. But we're not going to focus on that today."

"There are jobs everywhere," Meredith said. "A good worker like you is wasting time at the Ocean Vista. I know a lot of people in the area. I'm sure you'll find another job that is far better suited for you when your mom doesn't need you so much."

"She needed my paycheck," David said. "I screwed that up today."

"Oh, hush. Listen to your friend. Uh…"

"Meredith."

She smiled wide. "He's spoken of you. You're one of the nice ones."

Her heart beamed, knowing David had spoken kindly about her to his mother.

"I thought you'd be at work," David said. "Isn't there the Montgomery wedding tomorrow night?"

"Always on top of things. Yes, but I won't be there. Like you, I am moving on."

"You?" He glanced at his mother and then at her again. "Is it that guy you've been hanging out with?"

She chuckled.

Ms. Rivera looked appalled. "David! You don't ask people about their personal business."

"It's not personal if I see them together every day."

"It doesn't have anything to do with Mr. Cole." She turned to Ms. Rivera. "Is there any way I can help? I don't want to pry, but I know things must be hard right now."

Ms. Rivera drew in a deep breath as tears filled her eyes. "They say I'll be okay once chemo is done as long as I don't have any more side effects. My doctor thought I was going to need surgery today, but they got that all squared away. So, I'll be going home tomorrow. Things will be okay. Getting there is going to be hard. Especially if David is out of a job. But we'll manage."

"I know I have a few places I can recommend. Something will come up soon. In the meantime, I'd like to offer David a grant to help him while he's looking for a new job and to ease both of your minds."

"Oh, that won't be necessary," Ms. Rivera said uncomfortably.

Meredith cleared her throat. "There is a special fund for just this type of situation. Part of healing is being around people who make you laugh and who love you. You're going to need David. So let me help you get this grant so you can focus on just getting better."

Ms. Rivera's eyes filled with tears. She looked at David. "Didn't I say we'd find a way?"

David couldn't look at Meredith.

"It's okay, David. I am going to write you a reference and call a few people. You won't be out of work for long."

"You think so?"

"I know so."

Meredith opened her purse and pulled out a business card. She handed it to David. "My cell number is on here. Call me tomorrow, please. Don't forget. I'll be waiting for your call."

"Why would you do this?"

Meredith let out a quick sigh. "Just because life is hard now, doesn't mean it will always be that way. You can still reach for the stars. Am I right?" She turned to see Ms. Rivera beaming at David.

"That's right. Thank you very much for stopping by, Meredith," Ms. Rivera said.

"Take care."

She walked out of the hospital room with a little less emotional pull on her heart than had been there when she walked in.

"Thank you for bringing me here," she said to Griffin when she met him in the hallway.

They walked silently down the corridor and down the elevator when Griffin finally said, "You quit your job."

She was just about to push through the revolving door when she chuckled. "That's what you want to talk about? Aren't you going to ask me about Ms. Rivera? David?"

"I don't need to. I heard every word you said. Something tells me that grant isn't from the Ocean Vista."

"No."

"That was sweet. I'm sure they'll really appreciate it."

"I don't think David, or his mother would have agreed to take money if they thought it was charity. He still has his pride. A small donation to help him and his mother get along for a few months isn't going to hurt me."

Standing outside the hospital doors, Griffin looked around. He appeared more tired than he'd been in days. Fatigue was dragging her down, so she understood.

"I'm more worried now about you," he said.

They walked to Griffin's Jeep. "It's a job, Griffin. I have had many. I'll get another one eventually. Or maybe I won't. I have enough money invested that I don't have to worry about it. It's just a job."

He stopped walking when they reached the Jeep.

"What happened?"

She shook her head. "It was a long time coming. Edward came to work at the hotel two months ago. He's green and makes mistakes, and he expects me to make him look good. I'm just tired of the drama. Let's just go."

They both got into the Jeep, and Griffin started to drive.

"That's not what I mean," he said. "That happens everywhere. You're strong. You can handle that. Why did you quit now?"

"He fired David because he wanted to be at the hospital when his mother had surgery. It didn't sit well with me."

"Is that the only reason why we are here?"

"Of course. I feel bad for him. Them."

"It has nothing to do with what you learned this morning? About me knowing about Lucas?"

"You have known about this for seven years. But no, this has nothing to do with...our son."

"Maybe so. But I saw your face when you walked into that room. I can't explain it."

"Yes, you can. You've never had a problem saying

what you feel, and you certainly didn't hold back this morning when you were…rightfully angry with me."

"I wasn't going to say anything to you until tonight. But Lucas called. He's been anxious."

"You weren't going to say anything," she sputtered. "Why not? Here I thought we…" She waved him off and stared out the window.

"What?"

"Please just take me back to the hotel. You know what? I'll get a taxi. Just pull over."

"Don't be ridiculous. Why would you do that when you know I'm going there anyway and you're already in the Jeep."

"Because."

His amused grin annoyed her, sending her into one of her moods, which she called *bad Meredith*. Much like the episode earlier in Edwards's office. "Just…take me back to the hotel."

"I came back to Crystal Cove to tell you that I'd met Lucas. I just didn't want to tell you before…"

"What? Before we kissed? Was making love to me a line you'd cross if you didn't tell me? I was falling for you, you know. Again." She chuckled as tears stung her eyes.

"I am, too," he said quietly. "The longer I waited, the harder it got because of how I felt. I didn't want you to learn about it the way you did, though."

"Why? I wasn't exactly forthright with you for years. I wouldn't have blamed you for not doing it all just to spite me."

"Is that what you think I'd do? I was always going to say something. I just…wanted to be with you—just you and me—without…this promise I'd made to Lucas between us."

She turned and looked up at him, cocking her head to one side. "Lucas and the military have always been between us. And I guess they should be. It's who you are. And Lucas is part of us even though we never got the chance to raise him or to have him in our lives."

They pulled into the hotel parking lot, and Griffin parked the Jeep.

"Yeah, about that."

She got out of the Jeep and waited for him. "About what?"

"I should probably first tell you that I'm skipping the rest of the reunion," Griffin said.

"Why? Are you leaving?"

"I was always going to leave eventually, but it depended on how well things went here. I know I sprung the news about Lucas on you last night, and I know you need time to process it."

"Thank you."

"But I made a promise to Lucas."

"Promise? You're at a point where you make promises?"

"Are you angry I developed a relationship with our son?"

She clamped her teeth on her trembling lip, but the dam broke, and she couldn't hold back any longer.

"Just how much of a relationship do you have with Lucas?"

"We've been best friends for seven years, ever since he sought me out to tell me I was his birth father."

"What?"

"I know it's a shock."

"You've been having a relationship with our son for seven years?"

"Yes. We spend a lot of time together. He's the

reason I transferred to Hawaii. I wanted to be closer to him after he left the service, and that's where he lives now."

Tears she'd fought back with anger for the last few hours sprung free and flowed freely.

"You're angry."

She swallowed hard. "No. Jealous. You've seen his face," she said, sobbing and then she laughed. "Of course, you've seen his face. He's the spitting image of you. Or he was when he was a baby."

Griffin chuckled. "That hasn't changed. We're like twins. Rather, I'm an older version of him."

"You've shaken his hand. You've probably even given him a hug. I had a few short hours with him when he was born. That's it. I didn't want to let him go. But then I did. I'm jealous."

"You can have a relationship with him, too. He wants to meet you. That is the promise he made me make. He wanted me to come here and talk you into meeting him."

"Talk me into it? He thinks I'd need convincing? Why wouldn't I want to meet him? Oh, forget that. I gave him away. Of course, he would be scared of my reaction. He probably thinks I hate him."

"No, he doesn't. Let me call him so you can talk." He pulled his phone out of his pocket, but she held him back. "I'll call him right now."

"Not yet. Please, not yet. I want to meet him eventually. I'm afraid he'll blame me."

"He's not like that. Truly."

"With you. You didn't even know about him until he contacted you. I was the one who gave him away. He'll hate me for it."

"He was raised by parents who loved him. Sadly, they were both older, in their forties when they adopted him.

And his mother became sickly soon after. It was bad enough that he lost one. He ended up losing both."

"And he was left alone. Just like David might be if his mother doesn't get better."

"Is that why we were at the hospital?"

"I barely know David. He works at the hotel and I see him. But he's a good person. He's a good worker. He made an impression on me. He has integrity. He didn't deserve what Edward did to him."

"You are avoiding the subject."

She turned to him and felt her heart squeezed. "I know we need to talk about this. I know I owe it to you and to me—"

"And Lucas?"

She drew in a deep breath, feeling the weight of what it all meant. "And Lucas. But right now, it's about you and me. I haven't wrapped my head around it all, and I need to. I have all these feelings and don't understand where they're all coming from. I mean, I know where. I just don't know how to—"

"I get it. I felt that way."

"I just need some time."

"I'm not leaving until tomorrow. I really don't want to have this conversation with you over the phone."

She nodded.

"Thank you for being there for me today."

He pulled her into his arms. "I'm always going to be there for you from now on. Always."

CHAPTER 10

The room had been cleaned up, the bed made, and the wine bottles gone. But as Griffin sank into the bed he'd shared with Meredith, he could still feel her presence there. He *wanted* her there.

She'd walked away from him in the lobby, and he'd wanted to run to her and tell her that he loved her. He'd always loved her. How could all these years have gone by without him knowing this. He had to have known it was always Meredith.

Even when he'd been so livid with her after he'd learned about Lucas, it was Meredith. His love was masked with anger then. But he never would have been as angry as he was if he hadn't already had such deep feelings for her. Meredith was a part of his soul. He knew it now. Karen never had a chance.

His cell phone rang, and he quickly answered it.

"Don't you have a job?" Griffin teased.

"It's lunch time."

Griffin glanced at the clock and did the math. Twelve Hundred. It was indeed lunchtime in Hawaii.

"How did things go? Did you tell her?"

"Yeah, I told her."

"And?"

"You know how you keep asking me what she's like? She's a pain in the butt. She's stubborn, and she's difficult."

"Hey, you're talking about the woman who gave birth to me."

"I know. What can I say? It's easier to think of her as a pain in the butt who drives me crazy rather than the shocked and scared girl she is. She's afraid you're going to hate her."

"I sent you there. Why would I hate her? Did you tell her about my mother's letter?"

"Not yet."

"That should ease her mind a lot. Does she want to meet me?"

"She's scared, Lucas. She was a frightened young girl who never wanted to give you up. She's scared just like that frightened young girl."

Silence.

"Soooooo, does she want to meet me?"

He chuckled. "You are a one-note musician."

"You're dissing my music? It's better than that '80s stuff you listen to."

His eyebrows raised. "Whoa. You are going to have a serious argument with Meredith if you say that to her face. Just be warned."

"Yeah? I look forward to it." His voice was softer. *Vulnerable.* There were a few seconds of silence. "Hey, thanks."

"I love you, kid."

"I love you, too, Pops."

IT HAD BEEN A TOUGH NIGHT ALONE. MEREDITH WAS used to being in her house by herself. She was used to the sounds it made when the sprinklers outside turned on and the buzz that started when the ice maker on her refrigerator started at three o'clock in the morning. And yet, as she lay awake on her sofa because the bed seemed too lonely, every noise made her jump out of her skin.

Her eyes hurt from crying. Griffin had come here for Lucas. There was nothing wrong with that. If the situation were reversed, she would have done the same. She couldn't fault Griffin for that. But she couldn't shake the feeling that he'd led her on. He'd let her fall for him, knowing he was here for another purpose. It was never her.

When the alarm went off at seven a.m., she pulled herself off the couch and dragged her body to the bedroom to stop the alarm. She didn't need to look in the mirror to know she was a mess. Hosing herself off in the shower wouldn't wash away all the emotion and messiness she could see.

But loose ends needed to be tied this morning, and the sooner, the better. She needed to talk to David and make sure he got the money she was gifting him, so he didn't have to worry about working while his mother went through treatment. She needed to clear her personal belongings out of her office, make the calls she'd promised, and when all that was done, maybe she'd see Griffin before he left. She wasn't sure when he was leaving. The reunion wasn't ending until after brunch. But Griffin had already told her he wasn't attending any more of the reunion.

Later that morning, she finished packing her office

and loaded all her personal items into her car. Before she left, she had one more business item to take care of.

She walked through the hotel, feeling light on her feet for the first time in a long time. She'd loved working with happy people at parties where people were happy. She suddenly realized it had been filling a void in her own life where happiness was something she didn't believe she'd have again.

"Is everything okay, Meredith?" Darcy asked with a whisper, leaning toward the registration desk.

She smiled at Darcy. She was such a sweet girl. So much about Darcy reminded her of the girl she was when she was Darcy's age. Meredith hadn't just aged. She'd grown. She could see things now she never would have picked up on when she was Darcy's age.

"I want old people's sex," Meredith said quietly.

Darcy's eyes widened. "Excuse me?"

Mortified, she said the words aloud, Meredith's hand came to her mouth as if she could shove them back in without anyone hearing. "I'm sorry. That was completely inappropriate."

"No, it's cool," Darcy said, smiling. She giggled. "If you're talking about old people's sex with the Colonel, I say go for it. He's a hottie. But it's none of my business."

Meredith chuckled. "He is hot. More than he was in high school."

Darcy's cheeks flamed as she giggled and pretended to go back to work looking at the computer screen.

"Promise me you won't settle, Darcy," she said louder so Darcy would take her seriously. "It's sad when you settle."

Darcy glanced up and said quietly. "Settle? Settle for what?"

"Anything. I did that once. It only brings regret.

People come into your life, and you think you'll get over them when they leave. But you don't. Life goes by fast. You're young. You have no idea. Years go by, and it feels like a blink of an eye. Don't settle. If you want something, really want something, fight for it. Go for it. Give it your everything."

"Are you…did something happen?"

"Yeah." Meredith bit her lip. "I saw David. He won't be coming back to work here."

"I know." Darcy showed concern, confirming Meredith's suspicion that maybe Darcy and David were more than just friends—or at least, Darcy wanted them to be.

"Don't let go of something or someone you want if it means that much to you. Maybe you should call David. He could use a…friend."

The smile gone, Darcy said, "Okay."

With new energy and resolve, Meredith walked past the registration desk and down the hall with a mission.

She approached Edward's office, feeling the pit in her stomach fade with each step. When she finally made it, she knocked on the door and stayed in the doorway. There was no need to prolong this matter. Edward didn't bother to lift his head from his paperwork, the same paperwork he had been working on yesterday.

"Come in."

"I won't be staying."

"Suit yourself. But take these with you and work on them. I need them done by this afternoon. They'd be done by now if you hadn't gone off half-cocked yesterday."

"I believe I quit yesterday."

"I hope you got all that out of your system."

Each second he kept his head down, it only infuriated her more.

"I've written up a formal letter of resignation from my position for your files. It will make it official."

She reached into her pocket and grabbed the folded envelope she had prepared in her office that morning. Then she walked into the room and dropped it on his desk. Stepping back, she said, "I don't need a reference from you. I have enough experience that I know I'll land somewhere. We both know my pay grade was well above this job. But David is going to need a reference."

"Stop."

"Stop what? You fired him because his mother has cancer and needed emergency surgery. Did you know that David's been the sole support of the two of them for the past five months? David, this young kid, has been taking care of his sick mother, and working his tail off here, and you refused to let him go to the hospital during an emergency."

Edward seemed to ponder that for a second and then shrugged. "I didn't know that about the kid."

"He told you he had to go to the hospital. You know, in the few months you've been here, you've never reached out to the people who work here to get to know them enough to care."

Edward sat up straight in the chair. "If he had let me know that his mother had cancer, it wouldn't have been a sudden request."

"He needed the job. It's all they have right now."

"And now he doesn't have one."

"That won't be for long. I made a few calls and spoke on his behalf. They will be calling you for a reference because you were his superior. So, I'm asking you not to mess this up for him. Give him a good reference because he was a good worker. I've already given him a glowing reference."

"You can't leave."

"The hell I can't. And when I do, you'll have to do your own job without me."

"Meredith," he pleaded. This job was well above Edwards's pay grade, and he knew it. What was worse, he knew that Meredith could do it very easily because she had.

"I'm asking you. My job is on the line."

She folded her arms across her chest. "I feel for you, Edward. You talked your way into a job that was above your head. But it's not my problem. I have other…" She was going to say problems, but none of the things going on were actually problems. The chance to meet her biological son that she gave up for adoption was a gift, not a problem.

"I have to go. I wish you the best, though."

Edward stood straight and rammed his hands on the desk before him as he leaned forward. "We have a wedding booked tomorrow night. There are two hundred and fifty guests, and they will be in the banquet hall."

"Maureen has all the details. I trained her right out of college. You may want to think about giving her a promotion. And if you're smart, you will also give Darcy a raise and promotion. She's quite good and has a good future if she stays. Just so you know, as soon as I walk out that door, I will not be on call. When I leave, I'm gone."

"Come on, Meredith. You can't do this to me!"

She turned to look at him. "I'm not doing anything to you. I'm doing something I should have done a long time ago. I'm doing this for myself."

GRIFFIN'S BAG WAS FULL, AND AS HE WALKED ACROSS the lobby to the front desk, he stopped and glanced around. Nothing lasts forever, not even love. It comes and goes and walks into your life. Today, it was walking out of hers again.

"You're leaving."

"Were you waiting for me?" he asked.

"I cleared out my office. But yes, I was hoping I'd see you before you left. You said you didn't want to talk over the phone, so I thought we'd talk before you headed to the airport. You have to leave today?"

"I need to be back to the base in a few days. I have some wiggle room if I need it, but I'll be pushing it."

Meredith drew a deep breath and squashed down the tattered emotions she was reliving. Every attempt to open her mouth and speak betrayed her. The sob that was lodged in her throat threatened to choke her. Her knees grew weak even as her arms longed to reach out and right the mistakes of their past. The last thing she wanted to do was bawl in the lobby of the Ocean Vista.

They were who they were. Despite the love they shared, they'd built their lives without each other. She knew it, even if Griffin hadn't uttered the words. The first time around, he'd held her in his arms and told her he loved her before she'd been brave enough to admit it. She'd loved him right from the start as a fifteen-year-old, long before they'd started dating.

His gaze penetrated her until she felt it deep in her soul.

"I don't know what to say. I knew you were going to leave, but this is the part I've always had trouble with. I hate it."

He stared at her for a moment.

"I will let you know if I hear from Lucas," she added. "I mean, if you want to know."

"He'll tell me. I'll be seeing him."

"Of course."

She drew a deep breath and forced the envy that was choking her back down her throat until her stomach hurt. Of course, they'd had a relationship for years without Meredith knowing it.

"The tattoo was for Lucas. Inside the butterfly is the symbol for giving a child for adoption. It's hidden. Rafe obviously knew about the butterfly, but he never knew about the adoption. I never told him about Lucas. It wasn't that he wouldn't have understood. I just didn't want to share it with him. I wanted that little piece of Lucas just for myself."

"You kept him close to your heart."

She nodded, unable to trust her voice.

"Do you want to talk outside? Maybe sit in the hammock out back?"

"And what? Relive memories?"

"Only if we make love. No, just talk. I think it will do us both some good."

"There's a bench hidden in the dunes near the beach. If no one is there, we can have some privacy."

"Sounds like a plan."

"Come here." She walked to the front desk. "Darcy, can you stow the Colonel's bag behind the counter until we get back?"

"Sure thing," Darcy said.

A few minutes later, they walked the path and found, to her relief, that the bench tucked in a sand dune surrounded by tall grass and a wooden fence was empty. They settled in, and each of them was silent for a few seconds.

"All this time, I foolishly thought you came to Crystal Cove for me," she said. "How crazy is that? I actually believed that. I thought it was me, but it was for Lucas."

"If I'm being honest, I didn't want to come at all."

"I understand why you'd never want to see me again."

"Lucas pushed me. He wanted to meet you. But he couldn't do that unless you knew he had met me and that you were okay with everything. He doesn't know our story. I didn't tell him because I didn't completely understand myself. And he was okay with that until I got that stupid invitation to the class reunion."

She nodded and then drew in another deep breath. She couldn't get enough air. There wasn't enough air for her to breathe.

"Does he really look that much like you?"

Griffin laughed. "I told you. He's a mini-me. Do you want to see pictures?"

She placed her hand over her heart where the butterfly tattoo resides. "You have one?"

"Lots."

"Lots," she whispered.

She waited for him to search on his phone, and then he handed it to her. "This is on my boat. We go fishing once or twice a month. I sail up to the Big Island from Oahu."

"Really? Oh, gosh, he does look like a twin. He even has your chin."

"Yes, he does."

He took the phone and then searched through his photo album. "This one is of him and his fiancée."

"He's getting married?" She looked at the picture. "She's beautiful."

"Alaina is the light of his life along with this little

munchkin." He swiped a few more times and revealed a little girl in a flowered bathing suit digging in the sand. "This is Olina. It means a place of joy. And she is a joy."

"He's a father?"

Griffin nodded. "Which makes us grandparents."

She chuckled. "So, you *are* a grandpa."

"Yeah, the skateboarders were right. I'm a grandpa. But she calls me Pops. So does Lucas. He sometimes calls me Griff, but most of the time it's Pops. He called his dad, Dad."

Tears filled her eyes.

"You have such wonderful memories with him. Seven years' worth of wonderful memories."

"Yeah, they're pretty great."

"He really doesn't hate me?"

He shook his head. "Far from it. I never got to meet the man who raised him. His name was Buddy. Not short for anything. That was his birth name."

She smiled. "Really?"

"But I did meet his mom, Charlene. A wonderful woman. You would have really liked her."

"You met her?"

"I knew her. I used to have dinner at her house with Lucas a few times a year. She died a year ago. Both of them were older when they adopted Lucas. They were in their mid-forties. Buddy died in a freak accident at work when Lucas was still in junior high school. Horrible. It left Charlene shattered. Charlene died from breast cancer that she'd battled for years. After Lucas found me, she insisted I become part of their family."

"Yeah?"

"Yes. She knew there was a real possibility that she wouldn't be around for any of Lucas's milestones in life. You know, grandchildren or a wedding or holidays. It was

Charlene who encouraged Lucas to search for his biological parents as soon as he turned eighteen. It took a few years, but he found me. She was fighting cancer even then, and I think she knew his time with her was limited. She didn't want to leave him alone. There was no other family. I think she wanted to know he'd have family when she was gone."

"It took me a little time to transfer to Hawaii, but it was a good move."

"You didn't want him to be alone either."

"The feeling was mutual. But he's not alone. That's for sure. Alaina has a big family. Wonderful people. He didn't need me. There is plenty of love to go around there. So much so that his cup runneth over. And they do love Lucas."

"But he didn't have you. His father."

"Buddy was his father," he said resolutely. I can't replace him no matter how much time passes. But Lucas and I have developed a bond. I'm more of…an uncle or big brother he can make fun of from time to time, I guess?" He chuckled. "And he loves making fun of the old man. We're close—closer than I thought we'd be when we first met."

A tear rolled down her cheek freely. "I didn't do it to hurt you," she said quietly. "Truly, I didn't. I wanted to stop hurting. I was scared all the time you were in Iraq. I was scared you were going to die. And when Lucas was born, he looked just like you and I remember holding him and thinking if you died, he would be a constant reminder of the pain of losing you. I was young. Stupid, really."

"You were alone."

"Yeah. I didn't realize that loving him would keep you with me. I was afraid of the pain of losing you. So, I told the nurse I wanted him to go to a family with two parents who would love him forever. I didn't do it to hurt you. I did it to stop hurting. I squashed that pain away. I never pretended he didn't exist. But if I didn't see him and look at those eyes that were just like yours, I wouldn't miss you so much. I never dreamed he would lose the parents who raised him, especially not at such a young age. And you two are like clones."

"There is definitely no denying he's my son. I never had to see the adoption records or DNA. I just looked at him and knew."

She chuckled but it came out as a sob. "I don't blame you for hating me all this time."

"I did. For a long time. It was easier. Anger. But I can't look at you and hate you at all. I tried though. The first few days here I realized I never really stopped loving you."

"I never spoke up. I should have, but I didn't."

"What?"

"I never told you not to reenlist. I never told you I was angry when you did. I didn't tell you I was pregnant. I put all my faith in you loving me and me loving you and you coming home. That's all on me. I can't go back and change that." She shrugged. "I'm not doing a good job at this. You know, just go. Forget I said that. You can give Lucas my number, and he can call when he's ready. Just go."

"No."

"No?"

"Why didn't you?"

"Which part?"

He moved closer to her and took her hands in his. "All of it. Help me understand. Why didn't you tell me you wanted me to stay? Why didn't you put up a fuss when I reenlisted?"

She sputtered. "It was done. You already did it. Why didn't you talk to me about reenlisting before you did it? I thought you knew how I felt? We were months away from getting married. Months! And when you reenlisted, you mentioned you wanted to change the wedding date. Why would I have to tell you to stay with me unless you really didn't want to be with me?"

"Because it was your life, too."

"*You* were my life. How could you not know that?"

"No matter how compelled I felt to serve my country, nothing changed how I felt about you. About us."

"It didn't feel like it," she said quietly. Nothing had really felt like it since. When had she gotten this way?

"I don't know that it would have made a difference in my going initially. And I did reenlist without talking to you about it. That's on me. You didn't create the chasm on your own so I can't let you think what's happened is all on you. I had a part of it, too. But it would have made a difference after that if you'd told me to stay. I would have insisted you come with me and stay on base while I finished my tour. We wouldn't have been together initially, but you wouldn't have been alone. There were other military families there. I would have fought for us if I'd known it meant losing you. After that, I only stayed in the military because the one thing I'd wanted to love wasn't there anymore. By the end of that second tour, I'd finished my college degree, so I commissioned to be an Officer. I got promoted from there."

"I was angry. It had already been four years of me waiting. Four years of me waiting for you to make me your wife. For us to be together."

He sighed slowly. "It would have been different. But I was selfish."

"Serving your country is not selfish."

"Not giving you a voice in our future was."

A dull ache formed in the center of her chest and grew with his admission.

"I was selfish, too."

He shook his head. "It wasn't the same. You were scared. Alone. And I wasn't here to support you. Every letter you sent me filled me with your love while I was in that desert. We didn't have technology like we have now. I'm not sure how that would have changed things if we'd been able to email, text, and video chat on a regular basis. We had letters, and I thought things were okay because I was serving my country. But I didn't stop to think about how empty I'd left you. I don't think I understood that until I saw your expression and your reaction to seeing me. I'm sorry. I can't believe it has taken me this long to get to this place, but I am."

Tears stung her eyes, and her hands trembled. "Would you have stayed and resented me?"

He glanced away quickly and sighed. Then he looked straight at her. "Truthfully, I don't know. Not about being pregnant. Maybe about me having to leave the military. And I would have. Who knows. We can't go back and change things. Too much has happened since. I wouldn't have had you living on base alone with a child with me out there doing my job for my country for more than my next tour. That wouldn't have been fair. So…I don't know what would have happened."

He got up and stood in front of her. "Lucas will call you. He does want to meet you. He means it. But only if you want to."

A sob escaped her lips as she got to her feet. She'd

thought about it many times, but shame had always replaced the longing she'd had to put her eyes on the little boy she'd given birth to.

"Maybe someday."

"Maybe someday soon?"

CHAPTER 11

They returned to the lobby to retrieve Griffin's suitcase behind the registration desk. With any luck, Edward would still have his nose in the reports and not be roaming the lobby.

They appeared in the lobby and upon seeing them, Darcy pulled Griffin's suitcase out from behind the registration desk.

"I don't want you to leave," Meredith said. "I know I'm very late in saying that but it's true."

"What do you want, Meredith? Tell me."

She moved closer to him and fought the battle of fear and longing. She didn't have the right to tell him to stay. She'd lost that right when she'd sent off that letter years ago.

"I… I want…"

He gazed down at her. "Tell me."

"I…"

"She wants old people's sex."

Shocked, they both glanced at Darcy, who immediately clamped her hand over her mouth.

"Sorry," she whispered. "That was uncalled for."

"No, no, that's good," Griffin said with a big smile stretching across his face. "Old people's sex, huh? How about mid-life sex? Starting over sex. And then old people's sex."

Meredith laughed. "Or just great sex. Oh, God, this is so embarrassing."

"Why? You obviously told Darcy what you wanted. I wish you'd told me. I wouldn't have minded."

"I'm going to go…do something over at the Concierge desk with Raymond," Darcy said.

She quickly walked from behind the desk and ran to the other side of the lobby.

"Edward will be fuming if he finds Darcy away from the desk," Meredith said. "He'll get over it."

"Did you mean that?"

"You mean what Darcy said about old people's sex?"

"Yes."

"You bet. I want to make love with you every day until we are old and gray. Yes, I want old people's sex."

He scooped Meredith into his arms and kissed her on the lips with such passion she didn't care who was watching.

"Come with me," he whispered against her lips.

She gazed at him and tried to gauge his expression. Was he serious?

"And leave all this?" she joked.

"You love the beach. Hawaii has beautiful beaches."

Wrapping her arms around Griffin, Meredith said, "Are you trying to butter me up with paradise?"

He held on tight. "This is paradise. You and me. I know it. I feel it with every fiber of my being. I have never known anything more completely. We've lost so much time together. I want us to have the romance we had. What we should have had all this time."

"How can we? So much has happened since we were kids in high school."

"We may have been kids, but we were in love, and that love still burns strong between us. Look, I don't plan on playing fair. I'm telling you that right up front. I'll use whatever I can to get you to say yes. I love you, Meredith. I have always loved you. That is never going to change, no matter how many miles and years you put between us."

"I love you, too, Griffin."

"Then come with me. We can leave all this behind in the past and start new." He cocked his head to one side. "Hawaii. Beaches."

She laughed with a sob of joy. "You think the prize is Hawaii, Griffin Cole?"

"It's paradise. You won't find a more beautiful place. And you'll love being on the boat with me and Lucas. You'll love—"

"I was all in at 'come with me.' I don't care where we go as long as I'm with you. The fact that we have a second chance with our son makes it all the more perfect."

He picked her up and spun her around laughing.

"Meredith!" she heard Edward call out as Griffin put her feet to the ground and wrapped his arms tightly around her in a warm embrace.

"Save it, Edward. I told you, I quit!" she said, then laughed.

"You can't leave me!"

"I already have." She kissed Griffin and instantly transformed into a place that was so familiar and wonderful. His love filled her empty heart to bursting.

"When can we leave?" she asked.

"As soon as you say you'll marry me."

She placed her hand over her lips to keep from trembling. With tears streaming down her face, she said, "Of course, I will marry you. I don't want to live another moment without you in my life."

SHE CALLED TO HIRE A COMPANY TO PACK UP HER house while driving to the airport so she could get on that plane with Griffin. She wasn't about to let him get away from her again. Many hours later, when they were flying over the Pacific Ocean on their way to Hawaii, her nerves began to get the better of her.

Griffin placed his hand over hers as they sat next to each other on the plane. "He's meeting us at the airport. I hope you don't mind."

"Mind? I've been waiting for the three of us to be together for over thirty years. I never dreamed it would happen until you walked back into my life. You walked in, and my life was complete. Thank you. Thank you for loving me."

"I plan on thanking you as soon as we touch down in Hawaii. Just so we're clear."

She giggled with anticipation. Love had walked back into her life. Oh, how sweet life could be.

There was a time when weddings made Meredith sad. She'd worked on many weddings over the years and found joy in the happy people whose weddings she created at the hotel. But the wedding she'd always wanted so very much and never had made it hard to feel their joy fully. That is until she and Griffin stood before the Justice of the Peace with Lucas, Alaina, and Olina by their sides and finished what they'd promised each other when they were teens.

She'd had a big wedding when she married Rafe. But he never stood a chance. This little wedding at City Hall was all she dreamed of. That and the old people's sex they were practicing every day.

But this day wasn't about her. Today, her son was getting married.

"Nana?" The three-year-old girl with long dark-brown hair and eyes, wearing a bright-colored lei of flowers and a floral dress, came running up to Meredith in the tent set up for the wedding party to get dressed.

"I'm here," Meredith said. The child launched into her arms and gave her a big hug. Meredith's heart burst with so much love that she could barely breathe. "Don't you look beautiful today."

"Olina!"

"In here!" Meredith called out, still hugging the little girl.

The tall and very handsome man running into the tent scanned the area and found Olina in Meredith's arms. He made a face at the little girl.

"Next time you want to run off to see Nana, can you at least tell Daddy you're going?"

"I don't like my shoes," the girl said, putting on a fake pouty face. "I don't want shoes."

"I told you; you can take them off when you walk down the aisle with Mommy." He walked up to the two of them and scooped his daughter in his arms. "Thank you for catching her. She's a whirlwind."

"A joy, true to her name."

Lucas's mother had left Meredith a letter. Griffin's promise wasn't just to Lucas. It had been to Charlene as well. Charlene's hope was that Lucas would reunite with his biological parents and have a relationship with him to carry on what Buddy and Charlene had started. It was truly the most precious gift to Meredith and the scariest thing Meredith had ever experienced. But Charlene's words were clear and ones that Meredith intended to honor.

Aloha, my dear Meredith,

Our sweet granddaughter, Olina, is too young to remember me. Any more grandbabies won't have pictures with me. I hope you will help fill that gap. Help Lucas tell them about their Grammie. That is what I wanted them to call me. You can use whatever name you feel comfortable using. But from this point forward, I pass the torch from me to you. Tell them about me through Lucas. Encourage him to tell stories. He doesn't like to talk, but maybe through your questions, he will open up and heal and let his children know his Grammie and Grampi. There is never enough love for one person. Never.

I don't know why you chose to give him up for adoption, but I know that you loved him, and I know that it must have left an enormous hole in your heart. I want to fill that.

You gave Buddy and me the greatest gift two parents could ever have. Love him like you have always loved him from afar. Hug him like you never had the chance to when he was little. Remind him that we still love him from heaven when he is blue. Know that I am smiling as I watch over all of you on the beaches of Hawaii, and in the waves as you sail. I know Lucas will never forget us. But I find comfort in knowing that Griffin came into his life again. It's been wonderful to see them grow together in their friendship and love. I wish the same for you.

Our Lucas was never meant to be in my life forever. He was never meant to leave your life forever. Take care of the boys. I know you love them both so dearly.

Aloha is not just goodbye and hello. It's an expression of love, affection, and peace. So Aloha again, dear Meredith. It gives me great comfort to know that Lucas is with the two people whose love brought him into this world.

Charlene died less than a month after writing the letter. It was incredibly generous of her to be so kind. Meredith may have given Buddy and Charlene a gift, but they did as well.

Griffin walked into the tent and interrupted them. "Hey, are you getting married or what? The music is going to start in a minute. You don't want your bride to think you took off. We have to get on the beach."

Lucas picked up Olina. "It's time, sweetie." He turned to Meredith. "Are you ready?"

Meredith had been ready for over thirty years. She had a lot of catching up to do. Lots of memories to make. When she'd first come to Hawaii and met their son, his family and his lovely bride-to-be's family, he saw how comfortable Griffin was with all of them and listened to stories about where Griffin had been included in family functions. One day she would feel that comfortable.

Griffin had a seven-year lead on getting to know their son. But it didn't make her jealous as it had the day she'd found out about it. She was grateful. It made it easier for her to be accepted and included in this big and wonderful family.

Meredith looked at her husband and her son with love. "My, you're both so handsome."

"I want to sit with Nana!" three-year-old Olina said, pulling at Lucas's arm.

Lucas shook his head. "We talked about this. You're going to walk down the aisle in front of Mommy and then sit with Nana when you get to the end of the aisle."

She cocked her head to one side. "It's a beach, Daddy. Not an island."

"Aisle, not island, sweetie," Griffin said. "Nana is going to sit in a chair next to where Mommy and Daddy are standing. All you have to do is walk down the path to where Nana is sitting. Can you do that?"

"Okay, Pops."

A few minutes later, the music was playing and the two men she loved most in life were standing on the beach in front of an arch. Lucas's beautiful bride coaxed Olina to walk in front of her. As the music played,

Meredith took it all in and tried to figure out how she'd gotten so lucky. Love had walked into her life the moment Griffin walked into that hotel. And for better or worse, she wasn't letting go of that love. Not ever.

-THE END-

Thank you for reading LOVE WALKS IN. I hope you enjoyed the story as much as I enjoyed writing it. If you did enjoy the story, please consider writing a review on your favorite online bookseller's website.

For more books by Lisa Mondello, please visit https://books.bookfunnel.com/lisamondelloboxedsets where you will find boxed sets for my most popular series Dakota Hearts, Texas Hearts, Sweet Montana and Heroes of Providence.

To keep up on news and new books, please join my newsletter list at: dl.bookfunnel.com/zsuhh9rf7c and get a free book!

Many blessings,
Lisa Mondello